A View of the Lake

by

Trace Noir

A View of the Lake

ISBN: 978-0-9960227-8-1

Please also feel free to visit TraceNoir.com and MaskedWriter-Publishing.com for further publications.

Editor: Adrian Manuel
Editor: Cheriess Maree

Cover Art: Marta Dec
Author Pic: Demian Barrios (Back Cover Author Pic)
Author Pic: Peggy Sue Ruelke (Interior Author Pic)

Contents

A View of the Lake

Chapter 1

The Massage

Kaitlyn tugged on the heavy glass door as she entered the local massage clinic. Her cell phone, precariously pinned between her shoulder and cheek, was nearly lost in the forest of her long brown ringlets that bounced and swayed as she made her through the entrance.

She listened to her mother ramble on about her father through the phone. For a moment, she lost her grip on the phone and felt it slip down her blouse. Grabbing at her chest, she awkwardly put her hands on chest to keep the phone from falling.

Upon its rescue, she slid the phone into its familiar crook and sighed as she crossed marble floored lobby, decorated in dark woods and large bold trim. The air was filled with essence of lavender and spearmint. Light classical music could be heard from all corners of the room.

With her free hand she fumbled through her purse, retrieving a crumpled and nearly outdated gift certificate. Waiting customers glanced up from their magazines and glared at her and her phone, though Kaitlyn hardly seemed to notice.

She waived an offhand apology at the clinic staff. Kaitlyn's attention was divided as she half listened to her mother berating her.

The young receptionist looked at her with forced politeness.

"Mom, hold on, yes I know, hold on a sec. Yes. Just a minute..."

Kaitlyn plopped her purse down on the receptionist's desk and covered her phone with her free hand. "I know this is last minute, but I am leaving town and wanted to see if I could use this gift certificate today if possible."

Kaitlyn looked across the waiting room and knew she'd have to wait just like everyone else. But she was in a rush. She smiled at the lady in front of her, half-convincing, half-pleading.

"Will this be for a massage or a facial?" the receptionist asked.

"Massage, please." Kaitlyn said, a bit too anxiously.

Before the receptionist could confirm, Kaitlyn's cell phone rang in her hand. Kaitlyn sighed, realizing her mother had been on hold the whole time and likely hung up just to call her back. She was very needy.

"I'll just be one second." She rushed out the front door, leaving her blue leather handbag on the reception desk.

A young female massage therapist approached the desk. She looked at the gift certificate on the counter and rolled her eyes.

"G.C.'s NEVER tip!" she complained to her colleague.

Trevor stepped out of the break room to see what the commotion was about. He ran his fingers through his thick wavy blond hair, eyeing Kaitlyn as she marched back inside in apparent frustration. He noticed the way her dark hair swayed as she walked, and those delicate fingers of hers clutching her cell phone, the way she tilted her head, slouched her shoulders, and the way her breathy voice spoke to the reception... *'Perfect'* Trevor smiled to himself.

Kaitlyn snapped her phone shut loudly. She was feeling even more in need of a massage today than ever.

"Are there any openings?" she asked.

The receptionist glanced back at the young massage therapist cringing behind her.

"Yes. Just fill these forms out and we will get you started."

The massage therapist groaned as she marched back to the break room.

"I'll take this one if you want, Patty," Trevor offered.

The young woman felt reluctant. "Why are you so interested?"

Trevor smiled. He was aware his coworkers had the impression that he was not entirely interested in the opposite sex.

"Cause I want to leave early," he said. "I'll take your walk-in and you can take my 5pm. She always tips $20."

"Say no more," she said.

Trevor informed the receptionist of the change and asked if she would direct the client to the room while he ran to freshen up. He splashed water on his face and stared at his reflection in the mirror. He was just shy of six foot tall, fit, with broad shoulders and a narrow waist. He straightened the collar of his light blue clinic-issued polo before exiting.

Kaitlyn felt anxious and relieved as she followed the receptionist to her treatment room.

"Here's your room. Dress down to your comfort level and get under the sheets, face down. Your massage therapist will be with you shortly."

"Thanks," Kaitlyn replied, already tugging at her shirt.

Trevor opened the door to the dimly lit massage room to see his client face down on the table and introduced himself.

Placing his hands gently on her back, he asked her what brought her in today.

Kaitlyn remarked how her mother had been saving a gift certificate forever and never used it. She went on to explain she had been packing all week for a big move and that her back and neck were killing her.

"You are moving out of town?" Trevor asked.

"Yes, out of my parent's house and going to Loon Lake," she said, her words partly muffled through the face cradle.

"Loon Lake? Never heard of it."

"It's about 3 hours from here. It's a little resort town on the lake. Quiet and secluded. I found a great condo out there! I'm kind of excited because it will be my first time living on my own." Kaitlyn said, exhaling. She found the thought supremely soothing. Or the massage was beginning to work. Either way, Kaitlyn could feel pressure lifting off her shoulders.

"My parents aren't *too excited* about me moving," Kaitlyn continued. "They're still trying to talk me out of it. They don't understand. I just need to get away. Anyhow, I am gonna spend the weekend with them then drive over Monday morning to meet the movers at my new place!"

Trevor pulled her hair away from her neck and slowly began working his thumbs into the base of her skull.

"I'll probably need another massage after spending the weekend with my family. They *can* be a bit much."

"Did your job make you choose Loon Lake?"

"Hmm? Oh, no, I have an online business and it's finally supporting me now. I can work anywhere, really. But I liked the idea of living in a place where no one really knows me. It's close enough to be able to drive over and check on my parents, but far enough that they will be out of my business."

"Now you can relax..." Trevor whispered.

She mumbled something before drifting off.

Trevor worked in silence as his hands traced the curves of her waist. He replayed everything she said repeatedly, committing the details to memory. Kneading her muscles, he traced the line around her scapula and then worked down her shoulders to her arms. Nearly unconscious, he heard her moan as he gradually moved from her lower back and towards her legs.

When the massage was over, Trevor quietly left his slumbering guest and slipped out of the room with her file in hand.

Chapter 2

A Friendly Smile

Kaitlyn climbed the worn stone steps to her parent's front door. She paused, gathering the energy to face them once more. She opened the door and waited just inside, unaware that she was being watched from a parked car down the wooded road.

Trevor sat quietly in his car as he recorded Kaitlyn's interactions with her parents. A tall white-haired man with broad shoulders stomped towards Kaitlyn with obvious disapproval. A short round woman quickly emerged to dissipate some of the tension. Though he was unable to hear, he could interpret the tone. It seemed they were very unhappy with their daughter and not at all shy about telling her so.

Trevor almost felt bad for Kaitlyn as she tried her best to console her parents.

A moving truck parked along the curb was slowly being filled with Kaitlyn's belongings. Trevor rubbed at the ache on the side of his leg as he noted the name of the moving company, and the uniforms the workers wore. Trevor snatched up a map, marking the route to Loon Lake.

He followed Kaitlyn to her friend's small dingy apartment just a block away from her parent's house. She was likely spending the night there. Trevor was beginning to see just how eager Kaitlyn was to get out.

He watched Kaitlyn disappear inside the apartment, then, checking to see that the blinds were still closed, he embarked on the long road to Loon Lake.

After an early morning nap on the edge of town, Trevor decided to acquaint himself with the area. The village town was scattered with cedar homes, and old concrete and brick buildings along meandering roads that encircled the glassy edged lake. The water glistened in the morning sun, stretching out across acres and acres of water. Winding edges with expensive homes and condo buildings decorated the watery landscape. Trevor could appreciate what Kaitlyn had seen in this little out of the way town. It was small enough to feel cozy, but big enough to lose yourself in.

Trevor pulled into a gas station and sauntered up to the bushy eye-browed old man behind the counter. "I hear this area has some great lake side condos for sale. You know which ones are the best?"

The old man nodded. "The only condos worth purchasing are on the lake are at the far end," he gestured across. "Private residences on the left and a small RV park to the right. The only condos that haven't been bought up by rich yuppies and turned in to summer homes are the old ones in that bend there. Newly refurbished, though. I hear they are pretty penny, but worth every dime." The old man nodded his grey head at Trevor.

"Long waiting list for that place. It's got the best view of the lake."

Trevor turned to admire the view. He could see the potential it offered.

"Are you just passing through or are you one of the lucky ones who knows how to appreciate a small town?" The old man asked.

"I'd like to think I'm one of the lucky ones," Trevor said with a smile.

Chapter 3

Trevor

Kaitlyn unlocked the front door. The apartment was clean and newly renovated. She took in the empty space and tried to imagine how she would position her furniture. So far, she only had one small sofa chair. It would look startlingly barren, no doubt. But there were so many possibilities. She thought of how she wanted to purchase a new leather living room set once she was settled in. A bigger TV after that, with shelves and cases bookending her private entertainment center. She'd never have to leave this place. Kaitlyn checked the time. The movers would arrive soon.

Kaitlyn climbed the stairs to her master bedroom where a large balcony overlooked the lake. The room was large and spacious, a huge contrast to her former childhood room for the last twenty-three years. A walk-in closet and full bathroom were other luxuries she couldn't wait to enjoy. Leaning against the cold concrete wall, she gazed out the full-length sliding glass doors and felt comfortably at home. She pictured her things, her decorations, frames, and even the color she might paint the walls one day.

Though the walls were freshly painted, the recent renovations held true to the architect's original vision for the complex.

Quiet at least, she thought. It would be hard to hear her neighbors through the thick concrete walls.

She smiled as she thought about getting to know each of them, preferably over a glass of wine on her balcony.

A knock on the front door interrupted her blissful daydream.

The movers! She eagerly made her way downstairs.

A tall man in a dark blue polo shirt and baseball hat shyly stepped forward.

"Miss Hendricks?"

"That's me!"

The man was flustered by Kaitlyn's enthusiasm for a moment. He stuttered as he introduced himself.

"Before I have the boys start moving everything in, could you let me know which items you would like in which rooms so we can do this as efficiently as possible?"

Kaitlyn couldn't help but notice the man's blue eyes, calm and still as the lake. She found herself blushing as their eyes met.

Kaitlyn walked him up the stairs to the master bedroom and showed him her room. He paused a moment to take in the gorgeous view of the lake.

Then he followed her to the guest room across the hall. "This will be my office, so all the books, CDs, and computer stuff can all go in here."

The man nodded as they walked back downstairs. She

indicated where she would want her TV set up, along with her one chair.

"And the boxes labeled kitchen would, of course, be in here," she said, gesturing towards her kitchen.

Kaitlyn stopped rambling and looked at the man, "I'm sorry I didn't ask your name...I'm Kaitlyn."

"My name is Trevor. I will try to take care of your belongings as best as possible, ma'am...uh, Kaitlyn. If you need anything or have any questions, you can come straight to me."

Kaitlyn watched as Trevor walked out and began talking with the other workers, each of them nodding along and looking to him for direction. Everything seemed to be well under control.

Admiring the view from her deck she leaned over the railing. The water below rippled beneath as a pair of black and white speckled Loons zigzagged their way near the water's edge, gliding effortlessly.

Trevor took charge and made sure each man knew which room to go to. She had a lot of boxes, along with an over-sized bed and dresser set, yet Trevor kept the crew moving. Even managing to keep the men from banging up her walls as they struggled with her furniture up the stairs.

After a while Kaitlyn decided she wanted to see how her bedroom was shaping up. The movers placed her dresser up against the wall. Did she want it there? She didn't know. It would take her some time to decide.

Trevor approached her from behind and gestured towards two men ascending the stairs with her bed frame in hand.

"Have you decided where we should put the bed, Kait?" Trevor asked.

Kaitlyn ignored the fact he had shortened her name.

"I was thinking near the window…"

Trevor looked around thinking, "Well we can always move it later if you don't like it. But I think it might be better against this wall so when you wake up, you look right out to the lake."

Kaitlyn was impressed with his input. She couldn't help but agree. She decided it was best to stay out of their way. She walked into the bathroom and started unpacking her towels and rolling them into cute little bundles to fit decoratively on the shelf near the bathtub.

The shower had a small window looking out through frosted louvers. Kaitlyn tugged at the handle of the window and noticed it had been painted shut. Oh well, she thought. This would have been something her father would have jumped right in and offered to fix, but it was all up to her now.

Kaitlyn walked back into her bedroom to see Trevor setting up a nightstand next to the bed and placing a lamp on top.

"Don't worry about the small stuff. I can handle it." She turned and opened a box that read "bedding." She pulled out her sheets and comforter and began making her bed as Trevor stepped out.

She wanted to get her room done as quickly as possible. Feeling comfortable in at least one room was important to her.

Trevor came back up the stairs and into the room.

"The guys are gonna take a lunch break. They'll be back in an hour and a half to finish up."

Kaitlyn looked at the time and realized it was already 1 pm. The day had flown by.

"Oh, ok. Do you guys accept tips?"

Trevor laughed and said, "Well, *they* would, but it's not necessary. Just doing our job."

Kaitlyn looked around for her purse, finding it tucked away in a corner. She fumbled through its contents. No cash. "Hmm... I suppose I'll have to run to the bank."

Trevor looked at his watch and then out the door where the movers were lounging with their lunches.

"This is embarrassing, but do you think I could catch a ride with you to town? I just have to pick something up. It won't take long."

"Sure." She said tearing her eyes from his gorgeous blues. "I was gonna grab a bite too." She invited with a smile.

Trevor nodded at the invite. Kaitlyn scooped up her purse and headed out the door with Trevor close behind her.

Trevor turned to the movers as he got in Kaitlyn's car, "We will be back in an hour or so guys." A few of them waved and as they drove off.

Kaitlyn pulled up to the drive-through window at a nearby branch of her bank. She showed her ID and asked to withdraw some cash. The lady looked at her license and asked if she had just moved to the area.

"Today, in fact!" Kaitlyn said.

Trevor leaned in to look at the teller behind the window and smiled at her. "You wouldn't know if there's a Western Union near here, would you?"

The teller thought for a second and then shook her head no. "Sorry hon, I think the nearest one is in the Valley."

Trevor nodded in agreement and sat back.

"Where did you need to go?" Kaitlyn asked, pulling away from the drive-thru window.

"Just around the corner. A little motel right here. Just drive up to the front lobby. I can run in quick."

Kaitlyn stopped the car up to the front door and Trevor hopped out. Dashing up to the front desk, Trevor had some words with the receptionist. Kaitlyn watched him for a moment until he looked up at her. She smiled and quickly looked away not wanting to seem nosey.

Trevor returned to the car and then suggested a little café nearby for a fast bite of healthy Mediterranean. Kaitlyn agreed, eager to get to know the community and its cafes'.

Trevor was pleasant and charming, and she enjoyed his company. *Better than eating alone*, she thought.

They entered the quiet café, Trevor taking the lead. The diner was nearly empty. The waitress directed them towards a table over by the window. Trevor rushed forth and pulled out her chair for her. Kaitlyn graciously sat down and reached for a glass of ice water trying to mask her sudden nervousness. She reached for the menu to calm sudden nerves.

"See anything you like?" Trevor asked.

"It all looks good. Any suggestions?" she said, her throat tightening.

"Depends on what you're in the mood for."

Kaitlyn let out a nervous laugh. As much as she liked his attention, it was not something she was used to. How long had it been since she was last on a date? Too long, Kaitlyn thought to herself.

The waiter approached their table to take their order, but before Kaitlyn could reply, Trevor spoke first. "We would like to split the Garlic chicken pesto salad with a side of the salmon spinach rolls." He then handed the menus back to the waitress.

"Did you want anything to drink other than water?" he asked Kaitlyn.

"No, thank you."

The waitress giggled, glancing at Kaitlyn curiously before she dashed off.

Each of them picked shyly at the plate of Garlic chicken as they leaned across the small table. Trevor had dismissed the idea of an extra plate before Kaitlyn could accept it. Now she was forced to cozy up to her new friend.

Kaitlyn felt her nerves warring inside her. He was sweet, but overbearing, maybe even controlling. Though, she thought, he was also handsome and a much-needed distraction.

After they had finished their lunch, they quietly sat and gazed at the afternoon sky on the lake, stealing a few glances at each other when each thought the other wouldn't notice. An energetic connection obviously present.

Trevor excused himself to pay the bill without Kaitlyn noticing. When he returned, he remarked that he had better check on the guys and make sure they were getting things wrapped up. It was almost 3 pm.

Kaitlyn noticed he had the receipt in his hand.

"You didn't have to."

"You were kind enough to drive me. The least I could do is pay for lunch."

Kaitlyn blushed. Trevor nodded at the waitress as he opened the door for Kaitlyn and gave the girl a $20 tip.

She smiled gratefully at him.

"Hope to see you two again soon," she said.

"I'm sure you will," he replied.

Kaitlyn looked back at Trevor; his eyes focused solely on her. He was quite sure of himself, she thought. It concerned her, but only for a moment.

When they returned to the condo the movers were just finishing up with the last few boxes in the kitchen. Kaitlyn looked around at her new home. It was coming together quite nicely.

Trevor stood on the front step and assessed the stack of empty boxes accumulating on the small portion of lawn connecting the subsequent condo apartments. The offset design offered a sense of privacy from their proximity and shared walls.

Trevor's eyes followed the concrete path until he saw a face staring back at him from a kitchen window just four doors down. Trevor waved, taking off his hat and running his hand through his thick blond hair.

Once the shuffle of the workers boots, muffled voices and the clatter of boxes had stopped, the condo fell quiet again, still as the lake.

Glancing around the apartment she realized no one was there. The movers had all gone outside. Kaitlyn walked to the front door just in time to see them hop aboard the moving truck and slowly start to drive away. Panicked, she ran down the steps and waved for the driver to stop. She handed him a handful of $10 bills for them to divvy up evenly. The driver reiterated that it was unnecessary but thanked her for the tip regardless.

Watching them as they drove off, she tried to scan the group of men for Trevor but could not see him. How strange, she thought.

She stood out in the parking lot, watching the moving truck wind its way out onto the road, then she headed back inside her condo. *It would have been nice to at least say goodbye to Trevor,* she thought. *A friendship would have been a delightful bonus.*

Kaitlyn shrugged as she thought of her last relationship ending badly. She was not in a position to be dating anyway, she reminded herself.

After tidying up the last of her personal items, she poured herself a glass of wine and watched the setting sun cast an orange glow across the lake. It was now after seven and the sun had set behind the high wooded mountains.

She stared at her kitchen and the items scattered about. She didn't want to reorganize anything tonight. She would get everything organized one room at a time, her bedroom being the first.

Feeling exhausted, she closed the curtains that ran the length of her living room and wished her lake a pleasant night.

Kaitlyn marched up the stairs and glanced around. She saw an empty box on the floor that read bathroom and shower. Shower, she thought. Great idea.

The water was warm and relaxing as it hit her stiff neck and shoulders. Steam filled the room, fogging up the mirror as she stepped out. Wiping the moisture away with her palm, she smiled at herself for a moment before it fogged up again.

This was her beginning, her fresh start. A twinge of excitement bubbled up in her chest as she stepped out and found her night shirt and robe. She slid them on as she walked out to the deck, taking in the glint of light from the town reflecting on the darkening water. The town in the distance receded into the blackness, which made her realize just how far away everything was, or perhaps how far she had come.

Kaitlyn shut the heavy sliding glass doors, drawing the curtain for a close. She walked over to her bedroom door and began to gently pull it closed.

Kaitlyn stopped, noticing the hallway light was still on. She thought she had turned it off.

As she reached for the switch, a hand gripped her arm and yanked her into the hall. Another arm went around her neck as the hall light went off. Gasping, she pulled at the fingers around her throat. She tried to scream, but nothing came out. Her heart pounded with a heavy ache as she searched the darkness for an explanation.

"Shh…." a voice said, slowly easing the grip around her throat. "It's just me," he whispered. A second hand had clamped its way around her shoulders.

He pushed through the bedroom doorway and pinned her against the wall. Holding her tightly, he tore off a piece of duct tape and sealed it over her mouth.

Finally, her eyes adjusted, and she could see the jaw line of the figure in front of her. She threw an elbow, striking him square on the chin, causing him to wince momentarily. But he would not relent.

Kaitlyn looked into Trevor's blue eyes as she felt herself becoming dizzy. She did not understand why this was happening. He had had been so kind.

Trevor let go of her throat and Kaitlyn collapsed against him, coughing, and gasping for air beneath the tape. He pulled on the thick grey roll and taped her hands together, then shoved her onto the bed. Kaitlyn struggled to get to her feet, but he wouldn't let her. She tried to scream once more as loud as she could, but all that came out was a muffled cry behind the tape.

Placing a knee on her chest, pinning her down, Trevor wound a loop of tape around the bed frame then taped her hands to it.

Kaitlyn began sobbing and gasping as Trevor stood back and stared at her. His eyes seemed darker than she had remembered, his expression chillingly calm, almost amused.

He turned and locked the bedroom door, moved over to the nightstand, towards the lamp he himself placed on top only hours ago. Never taking his eyes off Kaitlyn's, he slowly reached for the lamp cord and gave it a tug.

The room went dark.

<u>Chapter 4</u>

Restrained

The coffee pot began to beep as steamy black liquid swirled in its glass prison. The aroma of its boiling trial filled the room. Trevor poured Kaitlyn and himself a cup, adding sugar and stirring them both. Trevor preferred his coffee with crème, but this morning he was going to have to do without.

Leaning against the kitchen counter, he stared at the sweet blackness in his cup. He hadn't been able to sleep much as she had been quite the fighter, he thought, rubbing his bruised jaw. There would be plenty of time to catch up on sleep. Now was a time to plan. Trevor carefully gripped the warm cup and climbed the stairs.

"Good morning, Kait. I brought you some coffee," he said as he entered the bedroom.

Kaitlyn buried her face in her pillow. She didn't want coffee, or to be near this monster, nor did she want to be waited on by him. She just wanted to be free.

"You look tired. Don't worry, I'll get us through this."

Trevor set the steamy cup on the end of the table next to her. He pushed open the heavy curtains to reveal the expansive view of the lake. He nodded and complimented her on her choice of corner unit and unobstructed view.

"Yep, I think we should keep the bed there against the wall. It's perfect," he said, abruptly leaving the room.

Throwing her head back in frustration, Kaitlyn cried out. The tape around her wrists began to tighten and pull at her skin the longer she laid there. The silence, the helplessness of her situation felt cripplingly real. The memories of him touching her in the night flashed before her eyes. His face, his smell. Her thighs ached from his abuse. It was all she could do to watch this man come and go.

He said his name was Trevor. He wasn't *Trevor* anymore. He was a *monster* with a friendly smile, roving about her apartment, her sanctuary, now her prison.

The grey restraints around her wrists were now mended and reinforced. Kaitlyn tugged and twisted at the restraints anyway. It felt good to at least try. The coffee sat on the nightstand, so close yet so far away. It seemed to taunt her as she pulled at the tape.

Trevor glanced around the apartment in search of Kaitlyn's car keys. He remembered her blue leather handbag had been tossed in a corner. He dumped it's contents out onto the kitchen counter, shuffling through until he found the key to her sedan.

Trevor liked her car. The leather seats were comfortable and molded around his body nicely. He knew he needed to act fast as the meager assembly of layers upon layers of duct tape would only keep her put for a few hours. A more reliable means of securing her for the long term was in order.

He checked the rearview mirror and was distracted once again by the bruise on his jaw.

Just a couple quick errands, since she would need special attention, he thought, waving at an old couple walking their dog.

Kaitlyn twisted and ripped at the fibrous adhesive that bound her wrists with her teeth. Pulling her feet up, she pivoted on her back. Firmly planting her heels against the wall, she pushed.

The heavy bed frame inched forward. She pushed again, crying in pain as the tethers secured around her wrists wrenched at her joints. She stomped her feet against the cold stone wall in hopes of alarming someone. The bed inched forward again.

Kaitlyn rested as she ripped at the tape with her teeth. The skin beneath began to show as it frayed, revealing the red bruised flesh. Tearing one hand free, she peeled and scratched at her wrist. She could taste the freedom now.

Kaitlyn bumped the side table and coffee cup along with it. The cup tumbled to the floor with a crash. *The cup,* she thought. The sharp edges could help cut her free, and... if thrown…perhaps it could break the glass, allowing her screams for help to be heard.

Kaitlyn scrambled around the bed and reached for the broken cup. It had cracked into three pieces just out of her reach. She pulled and struggled against the restraints. The small shards of glass and spilt coffee littered the floor. She willed away the slicing pain in her feet and pressed on.

She felt a surge of hope, stretching her arms and fingers as far as they would go. Her middle finger caressed the sharp broken edge of the cup. She took a deep breath and reached again.

Red fingerprints decorated the side of the mug as she fumbled with the largest fragment, gripping it firmly in her hand.

Footsteps sounded in the hall. Her mind raced back to the window and breaking it before she was caught. She raised her arm just as the bedroom door opened. Her heart fell, her breath caught in her throat. She thrusted her shoulder forward with all her might, but a hand grabbed her forearm mid-swing and the glass in her palm was launched downward, shattering onto the floor at her feet, her hopes of freedom along with it.

Trevor held her tight as she sobbed. He assessed the room and the bloody mess on the floor, impressed by her determination.

"You are bleeding," he said, quickly retrieving rubbing alcohol from a box in the bathroom. "Do you have Band-Aids?" he asked her calmly.

Kaitlyn didn't answer, hoping her excess bleeding may prompt the need for an ambulance.

Trevor rummaged through the bathroom boxes but did not find anything he could use to stop the bleeding. Suddenly he had remembered seeing a first aid kit in the trunk of Kaitlyn's car.

"Don't move," he said.

Kaitlyn glared. She did not find that funny. Trevor grinned, then dashed down the hall, leaving the bedroom door open.

The first aid kit was exactly where he had remembered seeing it. As he closed the trunk, he was startled by a young couple in tennis clothes standing on the sidewalk observing him.

"Sorry to sneak up on you!" the overly tanned-faced gentleman said, waving a racquet. "Tammy and I just wanted to meet the new neighbors!" His bleached white teeth gleamed in the mid-morning sun. "Name's Roger. Roger Putten. And this is my wife, Tammy." He extended a hand.

Trevor shook his hand. "My name is Trevor Manning."

"Somebody hurt?" Tammy asked, noticing the first aid kit in his hands.

"Oh, yes, my wife. Kait. She's ok, just a scratch but couldn't seem to find the band aids in the move," Trevor said.

"Just you two then?" Roger asked. "No kids?"

Trevor laughed heartily. "Someday."

"You know, tomorrow is our Park Picnic. That's what we like to call our little community. Why don't you and your wife come down to the Pavilion and join us? It'll be fun."

Trevor considered the invite for a moment. "That would be nice. We'll see you tomorrow."

Kaitlyn fumbled with her tender bleeding fingertips, prying at the tape on her other hand. Her feet were bleeding from the glass shards on the hardwood floor and began to throb.

Trevor waltzed back into the room, delighted. He sat down next to her and set out antiseptic wipes, gauze, and white adhesive tape. He cut the tape into short strips with small scissors.

"I met the neighbors. Nice couple. They invited us out to a barbeque tomorrow night."

Kaitlyn stared at the tiny scissors in silent disbelief as Trevor wrapped up each individual finger. He pulled her left foot onto his lap and began gently wiping the small wounds with antiseptic.

"It's a shame you aren't up for it," he said, frowning.

He pulled her left foot onto his lap and wrapped it in a towel. Kaitlyn winced. She jerked and pulled her foot back.

"I'm afraid you have a piece of glass deep in the pad of your foot." He examined her foot closer and held it firmly. "You may not know this about me, but I *have* been trained as a nurse's aide and was an EMT for many years."

The thought should have comforted Kaitlyn. But it didn't.

Trevor retreated to the living room where his own small bag of personal items awaited him. He quickly pulled out two prescription bottles and set them on the counter. The first one was a common pain reliever and the other a narcotic often used to treat the mentally ill. Together they offered the best answer for a situation like this. He took the hard white pills and smashed them with the back of a spoon against the counter and scooped the powder into a thick curry stew he had purchased while out.

Kaitlyn sat on the bed with her legs and feet propped up on a pillow to slow the bleeding in her left foot. Her left hand remained tethered to the bed frame, her right hand, now covered with white strips of tape around each fingertip.

She stared at the orange tinted stew. She was exhausted and hungry but had no intention of giving him the satisfaction.

He had left the bedroom door open. She could hear him moving boxes around in her office across the hall. She wondered what he could possibly be doing next. Finally, Kaitlyn gave in and fumbled for the plastic spoon. She tasted the curry. It was long since cooled down, but instantly comforted her as it filled her hollow stomach.

Leaning back against the headboard, she stared out at the

beautiful lake in front of her now mocking her as it seemed to slip further and further out of her reach. Her eyelids began to feel heavy; her body numb. *He drugged me…of course,* she thought, succumbing to the darkness.

Minutes later, Trevor found Kaitlyn slumped over on the bed. The bowl was empty.

Now he could work on removing the glass shard embedded deep into her foot. He rolled her sleeping body face down and pulled out a lancet and tweezers.

The sharp edge of the blade sliced effortlessly along the ball of her foot. A fresh stream of blood began to drip. Trevor delicately removed two large wedges of glass and deposited them onto the towel. He cleaned, dried, and bandaged the wound, then swept up the glass and repositioned the bed back against the wall.

Adjusting his grip around the power tool, he leaned forward bracing himself. This could be loud, Trevor thought to himself before squeezing the trigger. The power tool whined and echoed in the room as he sunk his anchor bolt deep into the masonry. Next, he measured the distance of the lightweight chain and attached it to a cable shackle with a small pad lock on each end.

Kaitlyn did not even stir from the sound of the drill. She was in a deep sleep. Trevor looped one of the shackles around her right ankle and pulled it snug.

He bent and kissed her lips softly, holding her image as he smiled, feeling very accomplished.

"Goodnight love," he said as he tugged the curtains shut.

Chapter 5

"Crazy"

Dear Mom and Dad,

I have settled into my new apartment, and I am loving it. I have a small confession to make. I have had a boyfriend for some time now. Fiancé, technically, and he has moved in with me. His name is Trevor. I know that this must be quite a shock. There's more. Trevor and I did not want to make big deal about our relationship, so we went to the judge and got married privately. I'm sorry it couldn't wait, but I am terribly in love with him. He is wonderful and handsome and the best thing that has ever happened to me! I think it is too soon for you to meet him, but when the time is right, I will bring him over to the house. Please take some time to process all of this. Trevor and I will take time as well to build the solid foundation for our life together like you two have. I love you. Talk soon.

Your loving daughter,

Kaitlyn

Trevor sat back and admired his work. He had spent the morning organizing the office and setting up Kaitlyn's computer. After several hours of digging and researching, Trevor had unraveled the workings of Kaitlyn's online business and was now replying to emails and running her business as usual.

Trevor found Kaitlyn's cell phone and listened to the messages, noting who had called. Then he changed her greeting. "Hello, you have reached Trevor and Kait Manning. Leave us a message and we will call you back!"

He printed out a forgery of the County District Court Marriage License, which he had signed and dated. He made a photocopy, framed it, and hung it above the dining room table.

With Kaitlyn's personal papers in hand, he called her insurance company and asked that an application to upgrade to a family plan be mailed to their new address, noting his name on her account.

There was a knock on the door. Trevor quickly checked on Kaitlyn who was still sleeping soundly. The knock came again, and Trevor dashed downstairs to answer.

A balding beady eyed man stood on the front step. "Good morning! I don't think we've met. I'm Bob, the complex manager and I have your lease agreement here. I was hoping you could sign it for me. I am just terrible with computers and the one your uh, wife, sent back, I just can't seem to open those things," he said, pulling the thick black rimmed glasses from his shirt pocket.

Trevor took the papers and glanced over them. "Oh, small change here," he pointed to the tenant's name. "It should say Trevor and Kaitlyn Manning."

"Ok. Not a problem."

Glancing back into the apartment, Trevor felt a twinge of anxiety. Kaitlyn could wake at any moment.

"Tell you what, you get those changes and bring 'em to the Park

Picnic tonight and we can get it wrapped up there."

Feeling flustered from Trevor's abrupt assertion, Bob rolled the papers in his hands and nodded in agreement as he stepped backward off the front step.

"Okay. I guess I'll see you tonight."

Trevor bolted and chained the front door and returned to the kitchen to prepare another meal.

Kaitlyn tried to move but her body felt like lead. Her fingertips were tender, and her left foot throbbed with every heartbeat. Her wounds had fresh dressings on them.

There was a paper plate of fruit set atop the dresser. Suddenly, Kaitlyn realized her right hand was free. She considered jumping to her feet, but then saw the additional restraint on her ankle and realized she would not get far.

The door opened slowly, and Trevor peeked in.

"Good morning. Did you sleep well?"

"Why are you doing this? Please tell me why," Kaitlyn demanded.

"Just Relax," he soothed.

Suddenly, Kaitlyn's memory stirred. She had heard him say those words before... She swallowed the lump in her throat as she tried to find her voice again. This was *not* some random act. Her mind raced as she put the puzzle pieces together.

This man had massaged her. He then followed her, posed as a mover, and kidnapped her.

Kaitlyn couldn't help but tremble. Now that he had her, what would he do next?

"We are going to be a family, Kait. As soon as you accept that, we can move forward."

"You're crazy!" her voice cracked.

Trevor shook his head in disappointment. He took a deep breath, then made his way over to the bed, perching himself next to her. Trevor leaned in, his voice deepening.

"If you *ever* call me that again, I will break your neck."

Kaitlyn held her breath. His words were loud and clear.

Trevor sat back. "How's your foot? I had to give you some painkillers last night so I could remove the glass splinters."

Kaitlyn sat quiet for a moment.

"Thanks," she said.

She was afraid of saying anything more, fearful that it might set him off. He obviously *was* crazy.

"You are very welcome, my dear. I also got rid of that horrible tape. I hope this is better. It's just temporary as well. Until you feel better and realize your love for me."

Kaitlyn nodded silently, trying to conceal her terror and sheer disgust for him. She couldn't tell one from the other. How could he expect her to love him? A shiver ran down her spine at the idea that she thought he was charming and handsome at one point. Did he really believe they were going to be in a relationship together?

"I have some errands to run. You rest. I will be home soon and perhaps we can spend some time together before the picnic tonight."

"What picnic?" Kaitlyn asked.

"The picnic our neighbors invited us too. This really is a great neighborhood honey, good job!"

Trevor was inserting himself into every part of Kaitlyn's life. Whatever was hers became his, and his became ours. It was suffocating. She knew the feeling all too well. She had hoped to never feel it again.

"They are NOT *our* neighbors! They are *my* neighbors! Stay away from them!" Kaitlyn shouted.

Trevor frowned. "Soon, you will see."

He left the room bolting the door shut.

Trevor had left a tray of food. It was the last thing she wanted to do, to give this man the satisfaction of eating something else he drugged. But her stomach was rumbling. After an hour she sighed and started eating.

Her thoughts shifted to her parents. It had been 3 days since she last spoke to them. They would worry if they didn't hear from her soon. They would come looking for her. They had to. Right?

Chapter 6

Attempt

The Rehabilitation Clinic smelled of antiseptic and rubber gloves. Trevor crossed the room to the small window reception desk.

A young woman looked up and quickly straightened her hair as Trevor approached.

"How can I help you?" she asked.

"I would like to leave my resume if I could. I don't know if you are hiring, but I thought I'd take a chance."

Trevor handed the girl a thick, elegantly printed sheet of paper.

"My wife and I just moved to the area. She works from home. I am more hands on, so to speak."

The girl wasn't sure how to respond for a moment. Her eyes nervously fell to the job requested line at the top.

"Oh! You are a massage therapist and PT assistant!" She scanned his resume further, "The doctor is not in at the moment, but I will make sure he gets this," she said, fidgeting with her blouse.

Trevor leaned on the counter, noticeably glancing down her blouse for a second.

"I'd appreciate it if you did."

The young girl fanned herself with the resume as she watched him leave. She made a mental note to request an interview massage from *him*.

Kaitlyn slept off and on throughout the day. Her mind felt numb. Every time she woke, she wondered how much longer he would keep her. Hadn't he already got what he wanted? She held back a tear threatening to form in her eye as she recalled the first night with him.

Apparently, sex was not all he was after. If he wanted to, wouldn't he have killed her already? Perhaps the real horror was yet to come?

She urged herself to get up. The shackle was just long enough for her to reach the bathroom. Sadly, she was only an arm's reach away from the sliding glass doors.

Kaitlyn washed her face with warm water to wake herself up. She glanced around the bathroom and saw the small window above the tub.

The bathroom wall was inset 2 feet from the exterior wall that led to the second-floor deck, making the window above the tub that much closer.

Kaitlyn tried to steady herself as she stepped onto the edge of the tub. The tether on her right foot pulled taught. She could only stand on the ledge with her leg extended backward to offer her enough slack to reach. She tried to balance on the ledge with her left foot.

Pain and the bulky bandage made her head spin. She reached up and tugged on the handle to the louvers. She cursed under her breath at whom ever had painted it shut. Kaitlyn pulled and rocked her body to and fro, praying for it to give.

She could feel herself slipping from her perch. With one deliberate pull, she let her body weight torque the handle free.

In one sudden flash, the handle gave way and broke in her hand. Kaitlyn fell hard, hitting her head on the shower handle.

She collapsed onto the floor of the bathroom and stared at the small opaque window above until the room began to spin, spiraling into darkness.

The middle-aged bank teller, smelling of jasmine and a hint of fresh perm, typed on her keyboard with long red fingernails that made an annoying click as she pecked at the keys.

She had a plump face with too much make-up and a smear of red lipstick on her teeth.

"Ok, Mr. Manning, your account is all set up. What amount will you be depositing today?"

"$40,000," he said rather calmly, and he produced two fat envelopes.

The woman's thinly drawn eyebrows raised, and she fluffed up her curled auburn hair as he counted the money out in front of her. She took it and recounted it twice before completing his deposit.

"Will that be all for you today?"

"For now," Trevor nodded. "Thank you," he leaned in and read her name tag, "Marge. You have been very helpful."

He sauntered out of the bank, enamored with himself as he smiled at the onlookers, knowing good and well that he had made the impression he had intended to make.

Chapter 7

Friendly Neighbor

Food, wine, and a genuine love for the two were important to Trevor. Many things in his life he could not control, but his choice of food and wine were not among them.

He casually strolled through the supermarket, observing the locals that eyed him curiously. He fondled a cantaloupe for ripeness and then slowly brought it towards his face to inhale its aroma. He paused, and looked up at the onlookers, most of them women, and gave each a gracious nod before choosing his fruit. He knew as his plan unfolded, he was growing more endeared to this community, any one of these women would likely vouch for him by the end of the week.

Making his way to the deli he saw an elderly woman reaching for her order sitting on top of the display counter, just out of reach. Putting on his schoolboy demeanor, Trevor quickly offered his assistance and handed the grey-haired woman her items.

"Here you are, ma'am."

The woman smiled in gratitude. "Thank you, son. Are you new here?"

"Why, yes I am. My wife and I just moved here. We were one of the lucky ones to get a condo on the lake. In the park."

"The park?!" she said leaning closer to hear him. "Well, that's wonderful. I live in the park as well."

"Really? What unit number are you?" he asked.

"Oh, I have been in 602 for nearly 20 years. Since they were first built, mind you!" she said with a flick of her wrist. Her fragile body slightly swayed towards him.

How convenient, he thought to himself. "What are the chances? My wife and I just took over 601. We are your new neighbors. I hope we haven't been too loud. Newlyweds, you know."

The old woman snickered and shook her head. "I haven't heard a thing! Of course, I take my hearing aids out at night. I sleep like a baby!" she said, grabbing his forearm to steady herself.

"Are you going to the picnic tonight?" he asked.

The old lady nodded. "I usually bring the deserts. Lemon meringue tonight."

"Lemon is my favorite!" Trevor lied.

"Me too! Oh, we are going to be great friends!"

"My name is Trevor Manning. Here, would you care for an escort as you shop?" he offered, holding out his elbow.

"Sadie," she said, taking his arm. "You can call me Sadie."

Back at the complex, Trevor dutifully carried the grocery bags for his neighbor. He followed her into her nearly identical apartment and placed her items on the counter. He watched as she rubbed her left hip and tried to straighten her curved spine.

"Are you ok, Aunt Sadie?"

She liked being called Aunt Sadie.

"Just getting old. Don't do it, whatever you do!" she teased. "It's not all that it's cracked up to be, that's for sure."

Trevor crossed the room and gently put his arm around her back. "You know, I am a trained massage therapist. I could look for you and perhaps give you some relief if you would allow me?"

"Now don't worry about me. It should go away in a few days or so."

"A few days? Oh no. You and I are going to that picnic tonight," he said gently rubbing her back. "Please, it would be a small thing for me. It's what I do as a profession. Hopefully I will get hired at the clinic in town. Please, allow me to help."

This was a tactic Trevor had used in the past when he needed to win over skeptical onlookers such as his boss' wife, a girlfriend's parents, or his own aunt, when she had questioned his motives. Doing a great favor, an act of selflessness always eased the conscience of those around him.

They were less likely to doubt him when they felt indebted.

The old woman was enjoying the attention from the young man. She had been lonely for a long time.

"Ok, but only if it is truly no trouble at all."

"My reward will be a slice of that lemon meringue pie," he said. "I'll let Kait know our plans and be back soon with my massage table, then we can get you fixed right up."

"Kait?" she asked, "I would love to meet your wife!"

Trevor sighed and agreed. "I would love you to meet her too! She is a *wonderful* woman. Unfortunately, she has difficulty meeting new people. She suffers from anxiety."

Trevor sat down on the mustard yellow sofa, sinking low into the worn-out furniture.

"I hate to say it, but I think she is getting worse. The move was supposed to be good for her. She insisted we get married in secret, at the courthouse. Didn't even want to tell her parents about me, though we had been seeing each other almost a year. It has been hard. I don't know why she even married me. She seems frightened all the time. I don't know what to do to comfort her or make her feel safe. I love her though, and I won't give up."

Trevor noted how Sadie was quiet the entire time. He had her right where he wanted.

"Sorry, I didn't mean to unload all that on you." He said, standing.

"Oh, hon. She doesn't realize how lucky she is. You just keep doing what you are doing," she said and gave him an affectionate pat on the cheek.

"Anyway, I really haven't had anyone to talk to about this. She is so secretive and suspicious of everyone I meet. But *this* has been nice. Thanks for listening. I'll go get my equipment and be back here in say an hour?"

Sadie smiled and walked him out. As she closed the door behind him, she felt confident that she had found a new friend.

Trevor climbed the stairs stopping halfway up to rub his thigh as it ached deep down. He panted as he continued up the stairs. He entered the room with a new plate of fresh vegetables, fruit, and a tuna sandwich. His eyes scanned the bedroom and then followed the chain under the door to the bathroom.

"Kait...." he said as he tried the bathroom door. It was locked. "Open the door."

Trevor waited for a response. "Kait, let me in."

Trevor shoved the thin hollow door open with his broad shoulders. The door gave at the latch as wood splinters erupted from the jam. He found Kaitlyn lying on the floor with a head wound. She was unconscious. The thin gash on her left temple had long since stopped bleeding.

Trevor rushed to the floor beside her and checked her for other injuries. He grabbed a towel and placed it under her head.

He began whispering to her as he dabbed a cool damp wash

cloth around her face, checking her pulse and pupils.

She was alive, but most likely had a concussion. The broken window lever on the floor told him everything he needed to know.

He carried her to the bed and lay beside her, gently stroking the cool washcloth over her face and through her hair.

After thirty minutes or so Kaitlyn moaned and slowly opened her eyes.

"You have been foolish," he said to her. "I never intended to *hurt* you. Yet again and again you hurt *yourself*. Why? I've been nothing but loving to you," Trevor sighed. "I am going to help our neighbor next door. I shouldn't be gone more than a couple hours. I'll get you something for your head." Trevor brushed his hand over her hair.

The crushed white substance powdered the countertop as he ground it under the rounded edge of the spoon, adding it to his formula. He scooped the white powder into a cup then stirred. He knew at this point she would not drink it willingly, but he was prepared for that. He produced a thin medical dropper and squeezed the rubber top as he lowered the glass tube into the tincture. The cloudy liquid swirled into the thin glass. His most ingenious cocktail, Trevor had to admit.

Eyes closed; Kaitlyn held her head with both hands. Again, she failed, and again she was injured. She knew she had to be patient and wait for the right opportunity. But how long could she wait? Kaitlyn swallowed back tears as she heard Trevor climbing the stairs.

He came bearing a cup in his hands.

"I have just what you need."

Though dazed, Kaitlyn fought and squirmed. But it was no use. Trevor shoved the dropper into her mouth and launched the warm bitter liquid against the back of her throat.

"You'll feel much better in the morning."

Kaitlyn let her head flop back onto the pillow. She knew he had just drugged her, but all she could do was wait until the drugs forced her asleep.

Chapter 8

Pleasant Surprises

The warm oil glistened on her skin as Trevor's strong hands moved rhythmically over Sadie's lower back. His body swayed and his shoulders flexed as he pushed and pulled at the fascia under her thin aged skin. He applied pressure to the deeper belly of the muscles and then loosened his grip as he maneuvered the shallow boney joints.

Trevor's hands formed a figure eight motion along her hip and towards the gluteus. Sadie moaned. He continued down the back of the legs and gently cupped the skin behind her knee, finally ending at her feet.

"There you are, Aunt Sadie. I hope I've given you some relief."

"Relief!?" Sadie moaned as she rolled to her side to sit up. "That my son, was better than sex!" Sadie pulled the thin sheet around her front and sighed a breath of enjoyment. "It has been many, many years since Herald passed, and bless him, he never touched me like that! I feel like I could fly!" she giggled. "Now help me off this thing so we can get to the pavilion on time."

As Trevor assisted the elderly woman off the table, he envisioned how easy it would be to snap the fragile bones of her neck.

The Pavilion was located on a terrace just above the small sandy area that dipped down towards the lake. Manicured grass and perfectly trimmed foliage lined the pathways. The low mountains and the setting sun in the distance were the perfect backdrop for such an occasion.

Sadie held Trevor's arm as he guided her down the stone steps, across the manicured grass to the picnic table where he carefully deposited the freshly made lemon meringue pie.

"Lemon again!" a voice called from behind.

Trevor turned to see Tammy Putten approaching. She was wearing thin white cotton pants that clearly displayed her tan lacy thong. Her beige blouse was loose around the front with small threads of glitter that caught his eye. Trevor inexplicably found himself looking at her chest. He cleared his throat and averted his eyes, hoping no one had noticed his moment of indiscretion.

He could tell this woman was not exactly shy. The way her hips swayed when she moved, how she delicately held her champagne glass with two angular fingers all begged for attention, not forgetting her seductive gaze as she approached.

She was on the prowl, and *he* was fresh blood. Trevor thought for a moment of how he might use this scenario to his benefit.

"It's his favorite!" Sadie exclaimed. "And he deserves it. He just gave me a massage! Fixed the hitch in my get-along." She said slapping her thigh. "Hell, I could dance the night away!"

Tammy raised an eyebrow. "You are full of pleasant surprises. I was just telling Roger that I needed a good massage. It could improve my back swing," she said biting her lower lip.

"I'm sure your back swing is fine," he replied.

Trevor watched Sadie make her way to a chair near the fire pit. She had found a whiskery old gentleman to tease.

"Those shoulders of yours. I bet you're strong." Tammy stepped closer and squeezed Trevor's bicep. Trevor slowly let his eyes rest on Tammy's thin frame as she inched closer into his side.

Unsavory thoughts swirled in his mind, but he held them at bay. This was not the time. Trevor did his best to go on teasing. He was following her lead.

"Perhaps I *should* have a look at that back swing of yours."

Her eyes fluttered and she smiled coyly, gripping Trevor's arm more firmly.

Just then Roger called to her from across the grass.

"Roger, come! Did you know that our new neighbor is a massage therapist?"

Roger stepped closer and held up a beer in salute to Trevor.

"Excellent. We need a good massage therapist in town. No offense to the pretty little thing down the road. She's nice, but I prefer my massage therapist to keep their feet to themselves!"

A roar of laughter followed from behind. Other neighbors approached and made their way to the fire pit.

Trevor glanced at Sadie now huddled next to two more old gentlemen.

"So where are you practicing?" Tammy asked, taking her place next to Roger.

"Nowhere, yet. I left my resume at the Rehab Clinic in town. I am hoping to work there since it's so close. That way, I could come home for lunch and be with my wife."

"Where is the little lady?" Roger asked.

Trevor shook his head. "No, she, uh, wasn't up for it, again. She isn't well tonight. She took a sleeping pill and went to bed already."

"At this hour?" Roger asked. "I can't think of any reason to be in bed at this hour?"

"I can think of a few," Tammy whispered. Only Trevor seemed to hear her.

"Well, let me talk to Richard for you. He is a college buddy of mine and the doctor of the clinic. He lives here in the Park."

"That would be great."

"Don't mention it. Besides, it would make Tammy happy to have you working around here."

He slapped Tammy on the butt then disappeared into crowd.

There were so many people around to entertain and he seemed keen on charming everyone. Trevor chuckled to himself. Entertaining everyone all at once means leaving an impression on none of them.

Tammy sliced a piece of pie and placed it on Trevor's plate.

"Apparently, you *deserve* this."

Trevor snatched her wrist and held it for a second before raising it towards him. He gently took her index finger and delicately kissed the tip where a small amount of lemon meringue had strayed from his plate, then released her.

"Lemon *is* my favorite," he whispered, then turned to join the gentlemen accumulating around the Fire pit.

Tammy inhaled with a flutter, feeling flustered. She scanned the crowd for her husband and then tossed back the remainder of her champagne before joining him.

The crowd consisted of Polo shirts, golf shoes, expensive cigars, and tumblers of scotch on ice. Most of the inhabitants were executive professionals, retirees or soon to be. It was a nice, quiet, upscale neighborhood. A perfect place for Trevor to build a solid reputation.

After a couple hours of eating, drinking, and getting to know the neighbors, Roger sat next to Trevor on a stone bench facing the water.

"Great, isn't it?" Roger said.

Trevor nodded in agreement "So, I hear you are a doctor?" Trevor asked.

"Yes, Psychology. I see the med-heads in town. A lot of screwed up people. Most of them here in the Park." He offered with a sneer.

"They talk to you, and you make them better? Give them advice?"

"Well, sometimes, mostly I make them less troublesome for the rest of us. You can't fix people. Hell, 90% of them don't *want* to get better. They just want their pills so they can cope." Roger opened another beer and crossed his legs. "Rich, spoiled, just looking for a fix. Others just crave attention."

"Do you do marriage counseling?" Trevor asked.

Roger turned and looked at Trevor. "You and your lady having trouble?"

Trevor lowered his head. "She's wonderful. She just has a lot of anxiety. And fear. I hate to say it's getting worse. She won't come out of the house, won't tell me what's wrong. She barely talks to me these days. I can handle it. I love her. I had just hoped this move to the lake would be good for her. But I..... I have another worry."

Trevor waited for Roger to press further.

Roger leaned in. "What is it? It's only half price if I have a beer in my hand...." Roger reassured with a smile.

Trevor allowed himself to slump, his eyes drifting out to the lake.

"She has been getting confused a lot lately."

"Confused? Like misplacing items or like misplacing days?" Roger asked, genuinely intrigued.

Trevor knew he had him.

Choosing his words carefully, Trevor went on.

"It seems like she has forgotten *why* she loved me. Other things too. How we met, our whole relationship really. Most of the time she treats me like a stranger."

Trevor exhaled for emphasis.

"Sometimes it takes me hours to convince her that I am her husband."

Roger cocked his head to one side contemplatively. "So, like an amnesia?"

"You tell me, Doc. I just want my wife back. I want her to be happy again. She tells me what she does every day and I know it's all made up. She is living in a fantasy."

Trevor ran an anxious hand through his hair, hoping to appear to be the loving husband at his wits end.

"I come home, and she screams at me like I am some kind of intruder. It's scaring me how bad she gets sometimes. I have asked her to see her doctor. After months she finally agreed, but at her appointment she seemed normal that day and didn't find anything *wrong* with her. Now she refuses to believe she needs help. I don't know what more to do...." Trevor put his face in his hands.

Roger patted his back, "I'll talk to her. See if she can come see me soon and we will get to the bottom of this. If she isn't *suicidal,* we can help her with some minor anti-depressants and regular counseling. I'm not cheap, though. I can't do it for free."

Trevor shook his head emphatically. "I can pay. We don't have a *lot* of money, but what we have means nothing if we are living like this."

Trevor made a show of glancing around the park at the other neighbors enjoying themselves.

"Please don't tell the rest of the neighbors. She hasn't had a chance to meet anyone. I don't want the whole town thinking my wife is going.... crazy."

"No problem," Roger said.

"Roger, dear," Tammy called as she descended the stone steps. "What do you think about inviting Trevor to join us for a soak in the hot hub?"

Roger turned to Trevor. "How about it? Great night for it."

"I don't know. I should get back to Kait."

"You said she was sleeping..." Tammy reminded him.

"True, but it's the only time I get to be near her."

Roger nodded his head as if he was already diagnosing Kaitlyn's psyche. "Of course, check on her, then join us. It will be good for you. Come relax. She will still be there when you get home."

Trevor looked up at the darkened window of the far end of the building. *Yes, she will,* he thought to himself.

<u>Chapter 9</u>

His Game

After walking Sadie to her door, retrieving his swim shorts, and quietly checking on Kait, Trevor followed the stone path down to the end of the row of apartments. Roger and Tammy had a terrace apartment that opened out to the tennis courts and the community pool. The hot tub was their own addition just outside their living room doors. A cedar privacy fence separated the onlookers in the park from Tammy and Rogers' little oasis.

Seventies music played in the background as Tammy stood holding an open bottle of champagne. Her white bikini glowed over her slim tanned body. She swayed with the music as she poured herself a glass.

"Come on in!" She welcomed.

Roger stepped out of the downstairs bedroom in a thin blue Speedo and greeted him with a slap on the back.

"What are we drinking, friend?" Roger Asked as he reached for a bottle of Vodka.

He poured himself a tall glass with a splash of cranberry juice.

"I'm not a big drinker," Trevor admitted.

"I don't tub with man that doesn't drink," Roger teased.

"Then I'll have what you're having."

"By the way, I talked to Frank. Got you all set up. He said for you to come in tomorrow morning for an interview." Roger offered, feeling pleased with himself. "He owed me a favor." He continued with a wink.

"Now it appears I owe you one."

"I'm sure I can work out a favor of my own," Roger teased, easing Tammy into the tub next to Trevor.

Trevor sipped at his Vodka in the hot tub. Trevor felt he was being tested, maybe even groomed. They wanted something; he could feel it. These people were playing *his* game. They just had no idea how much better at it he was.

Tammy poured herself another glass of champagne, dumping half of it over her chest, which Roger quickly jumped up to make a show of licking off.

Trevor laughed and accidently spilled his drink into the bubbling tub of water. Roger pointed and shook his head.

"I'll get us both another," Trevor offered, reaching for a towel.

Inside, Trevor poured himself a tall glass of water with three ice cubes and topped it off with a splash of cranberry. He wasn't about to lose control, he reassured himself.

Next, he poured a tall glass of vodka, ice and cranberry for his host and joined the couple, now passionately kissing in the corner of the hot tub.

"Don't mind us," Roger said, taking the drink with his free hand.

"Not at all..." Trevor said, easing himself onto a deck chair.

"Come back into the water Trevor," Tammy urged with a pout.

Once he complied, she threw her arms around his shoulders and began kneading the flesh. "Massage therapists need a good rub too."

"Do you go to the gym?" Roger asked, stretching out opposite Trevor.

"I used to. Massage keeps me toned, but I would love to get back into a routine. Are you a member somewhere in town?" Trevor asked.

"The Club," Roger said, swallowing the last of his second drink. "You like to golf?"

Trevor nodded, "I play a little."

Tammy let her fingertips skim over his shoulder and down his arm where it made a tiny circle inside his elbow.

She is trying too hard, he thought.

"Let me rub your feet!" Tammy giggled as she tugged at Trevor's leg.

She placed his right foot in her lap and began doing her best *impression* of a massage.

"That's a great idea!"

Roger chimed in, reaching for Tammy's foot. Soon it was a train of feet in laps, Trevor reluctantly getting Rogers' leg.

Interesting... Trevor thought. *What do they really want from me?*

Tammy slid her thumb between his big toe and second. The move intended to get his attention, which it did.

Trevor couldn't resist. He placed the heel of his other foot in her lap and pressed firmly into her pubic bone. Her eyes widened and she gripped his foot more firmly.

Trevor could feel that itch in the back of his spine. I wanted to show just how far he could take their game. He really wanted to test how far she would take it. A smiled tugged at the corner of his mouth as he thought about what he could do to her. They had absolutely no idea who he really was or what he was capable of.

Suddenly he felt Rogers eyes on him and hoped he wasn't as good a mind reader as he *professed* to be.

"Well, seeing as I've got an interview in the morning, I'd better head home."

"I want to see more of you." Tammy whispered as she followed him through the living room. "Roger won't mind." she said, biting her bottom lip.

Clearly, he wouldn't.

Trevor imagined shoving her against the wall and showing her how to really bite that lip, but he repressed his inner thoughts and nodded shyly.

"Later, Roger," Trevor called back.

He stumbled out the door and remarked how he wanted to bring Kait next time.

As he crossed the dimly lit path that wound its way through the park, he ignored the growing pain in his leg. He bent and rubbed it with the knuckles of his left hand.

"Ahh... Mr. Manning," the figure called out to him from the shadows.

"Yeah?" Trevor answered cautiously.

The apartment manager stepped forward into the light.

"I meant to give you the lease agreement. I was late for the party. Mrs. Rosen's toilet broke, and I was up to my elbows in... Well anyway. I stopped by..."

"You stopped by the apartment?" Trevor felt his fists bundle together. "And?"

"I knocked, but no one answered."

Trevor was relieved. "My wife isn't well tonight. She's probably asleep. But I can take those."

The overweight man hesitated for a moment. Something was off. He had hoped to speak to his new tenant, Kaitlyn, by now. He remembered how ecstatic she had been when he first showed her the apartment.

He wanted to know how she was settling in. But so far, he had only seen Trevor, a man she made no mention of previously.

Growing impatient, Trevor snatched the envelope from Bob's hands.

"Thanks, Bob. Good night."

Bob watched Trevor walk down the path and made a mental note to try and catch Kaitlyn, in person, soon.

It was all Trevor could do to keep from running the rest of the way back to the apartment. Upon bolting the door, he raced up the stairs to the master bedroom where Kaitlyn lay quietly sleeping, exactly how he wanted her.

Perfect, he thought.

Chapter 10

Med Heads

Trevor woke with Kaitlyn in his arms. A growing dull ache in his leg often kept him from sleeping through the night but today he felt rested and satisfied. Everything he wanted he had managed to get, so far. His plan was well under way.

Kaitlyn stirred and opened her eyes, she felt Trevor's' arms around her and shoved herself away as quickly as she could.

She sat up and glared at the monster next to her. Unfazed, Trevor smiled.

"I'm very pleased with our little community here. It's quite lovely. Don't you think, Kaity?" Trevor slid his thumb over the top of her hand.

Kaitlyn jerked her hand away. "Why do you keep saying that? This isn't our community. It isn't *our* anything! I'm not your girlfriend!"

"I'm sorry, sweetheart. You must be having one of your *bad days* again."

He patted her head and then made sure Kaitlyn's' restraints were secure before heading out for his interview.

It repelled her to hear him all her *sweetheart*.

Pressing her eyes tightly shut, she tried to shake the drowsiness away. It was another day. It could very well be *the* day. She lay quietly and listen for his movements until she was sure he had left the apartment.

He was gone…

Kaitlyn leapt from the bed ready to try again.

Trevor strolled through the entrance of the Rehab Clinic and approached the desk. The receptionist was on the phone, but suddenly distracted by Trevor's roving eyes.

"I believe I have an interview today," Trevor whispered, leaning on the counter.

She covered the receiver with her free hand.

"I'll let Doctor Saunders know you are here."

Doctor Saunders was a very tall thin man with white hair. As he approached, he held a clip board and wore a long white lab coat over blue jeans and a black polo shirt.

"Sorry for my appearance," he said, holding out his hand. "I spent the early morning with a friend at his ranch. He had a horse go down, and he called me to see if there was any way of saving it."

"So, you practice on Equestrian as well?" Trevor asked.

"No, not really. Just lending a hand. It turned out the beast had a minor pulled muscle. I had him put a compression wrap around the leg and walk him twice a day with no rider. He'll be fine. Our regular vet passed away about six months ago."

"Sorry to hear that." Trevor offered. "You know, I have been trained in Equestrian Therapy. It's been a few years since I had the chance to practice, but I could always be called in a pinch, for a friend of course."

"Wow, you sure *do* have the experience. You may even be *over*qualified for the work here. It would be up to you to promote and get clients. Of course, some of my clients will want to see you for physical therapy, so there will be some overlap. It can get pretty mundane." Doctor Richard Saunders said, tossing the resume on his desk.

"I'm fine with that. I make friends fast," Trevor said.

"I'm sure you do. How about you give my receptionist a massage this afternoon? We close the Clinic early on Fridays, so come back at 3pm. She has had *many* interview massages and it will be her that you need to impress, not me. Now, I must get to my patients. I'll let you know Monday morning. Be prepared to work."

Trevor knew the job was his. Making the perky blond receptionist happy was going to be the easy part. Keeping Kait from hurting herself or escaping while he was at work was going to be the real challenge.

Roger Putten was the key, Trevor thought as he dialed his neighbor's office. His receptionist answered and Trevor explained that he needed to speak to Dr. Putten personally before making an appointment. After several seconds, Roger came on the line.

"This is Dr. Putten."

"Hey, I want to thank you for that favor you did for me. It seems I may be starting on Monday."

"Excellent news! Shall we celebrate with some bubbly tonight?"

"That sounds nice. Well, I wanted to talk to you about getting Kaitlyn in. Last night she got really disoriented and hit her head. Unfortunately, it's not the first time.

"Last week she broke a glass. No big deal, but for some reason she didn't clean it up, instead she walked all over the broken pieces! When I got home, I had to pull glass from her feet and bandage her up. I am only telling you this because now that I may be going back to work, I'm actually terrified to leave her alone." Trevor paused, waiting for Roger's response.

"Worse than I initially thought. How can I help?"

"Well, I know it isn't your standard practicing procedure, but I thought you might make a house call? Since she is so against leaving the apartment? I know it must be *her* decision to talk to you, but perhaps if you and I were there together, she might relax and open. It would mean a lot to me. I would owe you *two* favors."

"For you, I'll do it. When would you like me to come over?"

"How about Saturday night? Say 6:30?"

"I can do that. See you Saturday night then."

Trevor smiled as he hung up. Dr. Putten had likely seen numerous Med-Heads, as he called them, in town and had probably made his diagnosis of Kaitlyn's condition already. Why wouldn't he? It was his nature.

Now Trevor just had to get Kait to say the right things, or nothing at all. *More drugs*, that's what she needed. The more disoriented she was, the better.

<u>Chapter 11</u>

The Ring

Trevor roamed around a small furniture store picking out a brown leather sofa and love seat and an elegant dark wood dining set. Then he found a pawn shop and picked out a thin gold band for himself and a diamond wedding ring from the display case for Kaitlyn. The clerk engraved it for a small fee. The initials TM+KM 9/14/2012 were etched into the interior of the thin band.

"Honey, I'm home," Trevor called as he climbed the stairs. Kait lay curled into a ball in the center of the bed. Her hair was a mess, and her eyes were closed. Trevor leaned in and brushed the hair from her face.

"Don't touch me!" she hissed.

Trevor took a deep breath and calmed his frustration. He needed her quiet and manageable before the furniture was delivered and the living room was full of strangers.

Dashing back to the kitchen he quickly snatched up the tincture and bounded back up the stairs.

Seeing the glass vile, Kaitlyn tossed her head away.

"I'm not gonna take it!" she screamed.

Anticipating her reaction, Trevor clutched her face and turned it toward him.

"Just take your medicine sweetheart," he said as he jerked her face closer.

"No!" Kaitlyn swung her fists at his chest.

Kaitlyn spat in his face. Trevor used the sheet to slowly wipe the saliva from his cheek, then he slapped her across the face with the back of his hand.

"That was rude, Kaity. You know I am just trying to help. I did not deserve that! Now, take your medicine."

With that he shoved the glass dropper into her mouth and plunged the bitter tincture into her throat.

He held her mouth closed, preventing her from trying to spit it out. Once he was satisfied, she had swallowed it, he let her go, caressing her cheek where he had slapped her.

"Now just rest. You will feel better when you have slept off this bad attitude. Then, we can have some fun."

The next day, the furniture store delivered the living room and dining set.

Trevor went about hanging pictures of himself and making small alterations to the house. He moved the small sofa chair of Kaitlyn's, out on to the deck, along with his massage table.

Just after 2:pm, Trevor headed off to give his interview massage to the receptionist.

An hour would be plenty of time for his hands to work their magic.

Tracy, her name he soon discovered, had only been in town for the summer to visit her grandmother in a nearby housing facility. She frequented Day Spas back home and absolutely loved massages.

Tracy was moaning and sighing with every tug and pull of her muscles as he worked over her back and down her legs.

He rolled her over, so she was face up, then he continued to massage her neck and shoulders. Tracy's eyes fluttered shut as he kneaded the muscles of her shoulder and neck.

"You are incredible," she sighed, biting her lip.

Trevor had grown accustomed to that look. Inch by inch the top of her sheet began to slide down her body, nearly ready to reveal her breasts as she slowly tugged at it with her toes.

Silently chuckling to himself, Trevor replaced the sheet and tucked it in snuggly so it would stay put.

A small pout formed on Tracy's face, but she said nothing.

Trevor ended his interview with a sensuous head massage, slightly pulling a few single strands of hair gently as he stepped away.

He had the touch. Leaving a client wanting more was his specialty.

But this wasn't the time for indulging. He had a plan and needed to stay focused.

Trevor quietly slipped out of the treatment room before whispering to Tracy, "I'll see you Monday."

Feeling overly confident, Trevor strolled into the kitchen and began whipping up a gourmet dinner of micro greens, seared lamb medallions, rosemary potatoes and red wine. A sauce of red wine, caramelized onion, garlic, and spices simmered in the pan as he lovingly stirred it to perfection.

Dipping a wooden spoon into the sauce, he tasted it, letting the flavors catch up with the aroma.

Nodding, he retrieved two plates and began dishing up the dinner, ornately setting three lamb medallions in a row, then a spoonful of rosemary potatoes and a splash of micro greens on the side. Then he delicately drizzled his special sauce over the lamb in a zigzag pattern.

Satisfied with his creation, he set the table and lit candles around the room.

Jazz music played in the background as Trevor stood back and admired his setup. The furniture was in, the table was set, and the candles were lit.

Now to just make Kaitlyn appreciate what he had done for her.

Kaitlyn sat slumped in bed. The cocktail forced on her earlier wearing off. Her head still felt foggy.

As Trevor entered the room, a mouth-watering aroma of flavors wafted in from below. The hollow pains of hunger gripped her stomach with a vengeance.

"Care to join me for dinner?" Trevor asked.

Kaitlyn tried to understand what he was really asking. She was hungry and the delicious scent of a well-cooked meal beckoned her. Though, she thought, the food was likely laced with more drugs no matter how delicious it smelled.

"What do you say? Wanna put on something lacey and come downstairs?"

Kaitlyn sat silently on the bed trying to decide what to do. As fog in her head began to clear, she wondered if she might find an opportunity to escape if he let her loose.

Trevor opened her closet and shuffled through the hangers until he chose a thin, light blue silk dress.

Kneeling on the bed, he caressed her hand as he removed the shackle. Leaning in, he kissed the red marks they left behind.

Trevor sat back on his heels and smiled at his pet.

"You are so beautiful."

Kaitlyn did her best to ignore his sentiment as she pulled the thin fabric over her head.

Trevor offered his hand to guide her out of the room, but Kaitlyn refused. For the first time since her kidnapping, Kaitlyn exited her room.

She expected him to lash out at her for refusing to take his hand, but instead, he put his arm around her waist and carefully guided her down the stairs.

Kaitlyn cussed to herself. It was her own fault that her injured foot prevented her from taking the stairs on her own. She winced with every step, and still refused to lean on Trevor's arm.

Kaitlyn looked around. Her apartment had been transformed, now fully furnished. A beautiful new dining set displayed a magnificent dinner arrangement.

Kaitlyn hated to admit to herself that he had done an amazing job of decorating her apartment. It was even nicer than she had originally imagined *she* would make it.

Kaitlyn fought to conceal her rage. This was her apartment and hers alone to fill and decorate. She gritted her teeth.

Trevor pulled out her chair for her. Her defiance getting the better of her, she promptly sat in the opposite chair.

Trevor didn't flinch but sat across from her and smiled.

Kaitlyn glanced at the front door. It was bolted, but it would only be a second's delay if she made a run for it. The throbbing in her foot reminded her that she would need to plan her escape more carefully.

She decided to play along. *Perhaps there was another way out of this*, she thought.

Trevor poured her a glass of wine and held his up to hers.

Kaitlyn held the glass in silence, waiting. He gently took her left hand and placed a thin diamond embedded gold band on her finger.

"You must have dropped this," he said. "Good thing I found it. I am sure you would have been devastated had you noticed your wedding ring was missing."

Just then a bright light flashed as Trevor took a picture of the two of them, capturing the shock on Kaitlyn's face, along with the terror.

"I got a great position in town. Decent money, I think. Enough for us to get by."

Trevor began to eat.

"I am concerned about leaving you for so long during the day. You haven't been well. Perhaps we should drive up to see your parents next weekend? It might be good for you. Cheer you up a bit?"

Kaitlyn sat listening in awed horror as she stared at the ring. She didn't recall saying *I do*. She realized it didn't matter. This man was convinced that not only were they together, but also married. *He is deranged, a total delusional nut job. The worst ones,* she feared. *So unpredictable.*

Trevor had released her shackles only to put on another. The color drained from her face. She wanted to bolt for the door right then and there.

"My…my parents?" Kaitlyn asked, mortified.

"Yes. You haven't seen them since we moved. I'm sure they would appreciate a visit." Trevor chewed on his food happily.

Nothing seemed out of the ordinary to him, Kaitlyn mused.

"I do want to see my parents. More than anything."

Just not with you, she thought.

Trevor reached across the table and patted her hand. The gesture made her want to scream, but she swallowed her voice and tried to appear as agreeable as possible.

"Great! I will let them know we are coming."

Suddenly Kaitlyn's gaze noticed a frame on the wall. A framed marriage license with her name and Trevor's name, hung innocently just out of her reach. Her signature perfectly forged under her printed name.

Kaitlyn's' head began to spin.

"Eat, darling. You look a little pale." Trevor held up the fork for her to take.

Kaitlyn took the fork, contemplating stabbing him with it and charging for the door. Nothing would please her more, but again she decided against it. She needed a better moment, one that would allow her more time to hobble to the door.

A delicious mouthful of rosemary potatoes revived her spirits. Focusing on her plate allowed her to avoid looking at him as she ate.

Trevor chattered on about his day and how he wished she had gone with him to pick out the furniture. He was talking as if she wasn't his prisoner, but a partner. She knew it was all the same to him. Every attack he made had been laced with sweet kisses and praise.

What did he really want? She gripped her fork a little tighter.

"Where did you learn to cook so well?" she asked with forced politeness.

"My grandmother." he said with a broad smile. "She was my only family, really." Trevor held up his wine in a toasting gesture. "To Gram," he said clinking his glass to hers.

Kaitlyn glanced at the wine. She assumed it had been tainted with more sleeping pills. It was her knew normal. Eat, sleep, eat and sleep some more.

Suddenly, Trevor stood and produced an eye dropper of his favorite pharmaceutical cocktail. He held it up to her mouth.

Kaitlyn backed away, refusing to take it.

"Please don't make me take that. I hate it. Please." Kaitlyn begged.

"Sweetheart. You know you are not well. Please, take your medicine like a good girl. I don't like having to force you. It's not fun to always be the *bad guy*." He knelt in front her to meet eye to eye. "You know I only force you to do what's best for you."

Kaitlyn swallowed the lump forming in her throat. Shame and anger warred within.

"I know you don't like being forced." he said in a soothing tone as he ran a hand down her back.

"It's not fun being drugged either," Kaitlyn shot back.

Trevor lowered the dropper.

"I made you an appointment to see Dr. Putten tomorrow. He's coming to the apartment. He will talk to you about your condition. If he thinks you don't need this, then fine. You can stop. But if he recommends you take it, then you'll *have* to. It's for your own good." Trevor held the dropper up for her to see. "I only want what's best for you, Kait."

Kaitlyn stared at the thin glass vile in front of her. She realized she would end up drugged again either way. After a few seconds, Kaitlyn took the liquid and made a show of drinking it, leaving a quarter in the dropper, and tossing it on the table.

"Good girl," Trevor said. "I have a surprise for you."

Kaitlyn glanced around the room nervously.

Trevor opened the curtain revealing the deck. Sliding the heavy glass door to the side, he revealed a massage table set up with sheets and oil and even a few rose petals for decoration.

Kaitlyn watched as Trevor began lighting the candles on the deck. The moon and the neighboring lights glistened on the water beyond.

"Let me take care of you."

He turned off the dining room lights. He crossed the room and swooped up Kaitlyn out of her chair. She yelped and tried to pull free of his grip as he carried her to the massage table. He laid her down, pushing her arms to her sides.

She didn't want a massage from him. He was the last person on earth she wanted touching her.

Kaitlyn suddenly found the courage to scream, but before her lungs could carry the sound from her throat, Trevor put his hand over her mouth.

Towering over her, he shook his head in a warning. Then he placed a thin cloth over her face and shoved the fabric between her teeth and tied it firmly behind her head.

"Relax. I'm not gonna hurt you. Just breathe."

Kaitlyn could feel her whole-body trembling. She had endured so much already, yet his touch in a simple massage might be her undoing.

Squeezing warm coconut oil into his hands, he began massaging her arms and then neck running his fingers roughly through her hair. Kaitlyn tried to focus her mind on what her next move should be, but the effects of the drugs had begun to dull her senses.

Kaitlyn once again tried to scream, but her voice was lost in the fabric.

Kaitlyn felt her skin warm as a wave of tingling sensations pricked up her spine and then melted like hot butter dripping down her sides as it washed over her from her feet to her chest and from her fingertips to her neck.

Trevor lifted her into his arms and crossed the room, lowering himself down on the sofa. He slowly glided his hand over her shoulder and across her neck and then down her chest between her breasts.

The caressing touch of his fingertips began to intensify as the drugs in her system amplified every sensation. She swallowed hard and tried to understand what she was experiencing. This man was dangerous, yet his touch seemed to intoxicate her.

Trevor gripped the front of her thigh and squeezed, then gently let the side of his thumb brush over the silky skin.

What is wrong with me, she screamed to herself. *Why can't I make it stop?!*

Trevor's 'Love Cocktail' was working better than expected. It was a mixture of ecstasy, Hydrocodone, and a hint of Prozac.

This was much easier, he thought to himself.

Chapter 12

Issues

The doorbell rang right on schedule. Dr. Putten had many faults, some even quite questionable, but being late was not one of them. He was a punctual man.

Trevor opened the door and welcomed Roger into the apartment.

"Where's Kait?" Roger asked.

Trevor nodded upstairs. "I had to be by her side all day today. She is having one of her *bad days*," he said solemnly.

"I see. And what do her bad days consist of?" Roger helped himself over toward the couch.

Trevor gestured and the two men sat in the living room facing each other.

"Well, she is often paranoid. She says she is a prisoner in her own house. She says that I am the reason she is unhappy. She has even accused me of locking her up or being a *monster*. Her *really* bad days, she doesn't even know me. Says she has never seen me before. I still don't know what to make of it."

Trevor buried his face in his hands.

"It's like she has lost her mind or something.... Do you think she could have intermittent amnesia?"

Dr. Putten pondered for a moment, he really needed to see Kait for himself before a diagnosis could be confirmed. Though everything Trevor conveyed seemed right on point, almost too on point with mental illness. Trevor leaned forward, looking hopeful.

Roger waved a hand in the air. "Before I say anything, I have to see her."

"Of course. She's in bed... as usual." Trevor then guided Roger up the stairs.

Trevor knocked on the bedroom door as he turned the handle.

"Babe? Dr. Putten is here to see you. Remember he was coming today?"

Trevor pushed the door open to reveal Kaitlyn half asleep and sprawled out on the bed. Her hair was disheveled, and dark circles hung under her eyes. Her shackles had been removed, and Trevor had applied concealer to the thin red lines around her wrists wear they had been. No evidence of her plight remained.

"Is she on something?" Dr. Putten asked.

Trevor flinched.

"Whatever she takes all the time. Her last doctor put her on sleeping pills, but I'm afraid she's taking too many." He shook his head in feigned ignorance.

Roger sat on the bed next to Kaitlyn and took her hand in his.

"Kait? Kaitlyn, can you hear me? My name is Doctor Putten. I am here to talk to you. I want to help you feel better, ok? I want to make sure you feel safe," he said, patting her hand.

Kaitlyn stirred and tried to raise her head. Opening a bloodshot eye, she looked up at the stranger leaning over her.

She swallowed hard, trying to find the words to say. Her restraints were gone, and this man claimed to be a doctor wanting to *help* her. Kaitlyn felt her heart flutter with relief and excitement. She was being rescued.

She stammered, the thoughts flooding her brain, not even one coming to surface.

Her heart fell deeper than it had ever been as Trevor quickly appeared by her side. He helped her up to a sitting position while lovingly putting his arm around her.

"Kaity, can you talk to Dr. Putten?"

Kaitlyn mumbled as her desperation bubbled to the surface.

"What's that, sweetie?"

She wanted to tell this man how she had been held against her will, how Trevor had abused, how he had drugged her and had taken over her life.

"No," Kaitlyn found herself saying. "No, no, no," she repeated.

Roger sighed, looking at the pitiful spectacle. He could only give an educated guess of her condition. He had seen aspects of this many times in his career and suspected his diagnosis was fairly accurate, but following protocol, he needed to see just how deep the mental damage lie for himself.

She likely needed more help than he could give, he thought as he watched what appeared to be a mental train wreck in front of him. He hated to dismiss her so quickly, but from what Trevor mentioned and her current state, it seemed quite apparent.

"Kaitlyn. I just need you to answer a few questions for me. Can you do that?"

Kaitlyn nodded, the tears racing down her cheek.

"Do you know where you are?"

"My apartment," she answered.

"And your name?"

"Kaitlyn Harris," she whispered. "Help me?"

"Yes, I am here to help you. And can you tell me who this man is?"

Kaitlyn rolled her head to the side, struggling to keep upright. Her gaze fell on Trevor.

"Bad man," she managed to say, her eyes suddenly filled with hatred. "a monster!"

Trevor rubbed her shoulder and kissed the top of her head.

"Baby, don't say that. You know I want to help you. I would do anything for you."

Kaitlyn pulled away from Trevor's constant petting and looked Dr. Putten square in the eye.

"Get me out of here! He has held me here. I don't know him! I can't leave this bed! Chains!"

She pointed to the spot where her shackles had been bolted to the wall, then glanced back at her wrists and feet now free and began to sob.

Roger looked from Kait to Trevor and then back to Kait.

"Do you remember your wedding day? Kait, look at your husband and tell me if you remember marrying this man?"

Kait stifled a sob and glared at Trevor.

"I would never marry a monster."

Putten nodded his head. "Why do you call him a monster? Does he not love you unconditionally?"

Trevor subconsciously held his breath as he watched the drugs skew her answers. With the right questions she could blow his cover or nail it home.

Trevor slid his hand over the syringe in his pocket. A form of Rohypnol. As a former paramedic, Trevor had acquired an untraceable amount of the drug. Trevor prepared to inject Dr. Putten if Kaitlyn veered off topic.

Suddenly, Trevor imagined the whole scene going bad, his course of action, and the ultimate demise of Dr. Putten in the worst-case scenario. The lake below might have to serve another purpose.

"He says he loves me all the time," she said.

"When was the last time he told you he loved you?"

Her head bobbed and swayed, and her eyes closed as she recalled.

"Last night. At dinner. We had dinner downstairs. He said he loved me, and he made me dinner."

"Focus on that moment. What else did he say?"

"He found my wedding ring. He had a surprise for me."

Kaitlyn squinted, fighting the drugs and the numbness.

"Good, good. And what was the surprise?" Dr. Putten probed.

"He gave me a massage."

"Did he hurt you at all?"

Kaitlyn shook her head, the confusion racking her brain.

"And then what happened?"

"He kissed me." Kaitlyn began to sob uncontrollably. She had so much to tell this man but only her pitiful cries could tell her story.

Dr. Putten took a breath as he assessed the situation. He sensed something wasn't adding up but couldn't put his finger on it. Trevor didn't appear to be an abusive husband and wouldn't have asked for help if he had.

Glancing at Kaitlyn's wrists, he wondered if he was seeing some redness or discoloration.

"Ok, I think perhaps you have just been a little confused. Your husband loves you and is doing his best to take care of you. Do you know why I am here?"

"To save me?"

Roger smiled. "Save you from what?"

Her hand stretched out toward Trevor who was now standing behind Doctor Putten.

"Him!"

Doctor Putten glanced around the room, seeing no obvious signs of a struggle. Only a caring husband and a very confused young lady.

Roger sighed as he stood up and asked Trevor to follow him down to the living room.

Trevor slumped into the side chair and dropped his head to his hands in a show of desperation.

Roger moved closer and put his hand on Trevor's shoulder.

"I hate to say it, but she doesn't have a memory problem."

"No?"

"She is showing signs of paranoid schizophrenia. I am surprised you have managed this long on your own."

Trevor shook his head, feigning denial.

"The best place for her… is a mental care facility. Just for observation, at least until we can get her medication under control."

"I don't want to put her in some facility. I want to take care of her myself."

Roger patted Trevor on the back.

"That is very noble of you but please consider it."

Dr. Putten wondered if Trevor's' insistence about Kaitlyn being home and under his care, might perhaps be some sort of control aspect. As quickly as the thought surfaced, he disregarded.

He reached inside his jacket and pulled out a white block of paper and began scribbling on it.

"Here is a prescription for some anti-psychotics. They may also keep her slightly sedated, so perhaps eliminate whatever sleeping pill she is taking for now."

He scribbled another prescription and tore it off and shoved the small tablet back into his jacket and reached for the door.

"A facility is best. It really is."

"I will let you know if it ever comes to that. I was planning on taking her to see her parents this weekend. Maybe they can help?"

"I am gonna give you this too. It's a prescription for a light sedative to help you sleep." He handed Trevor the prescription.

Trevor nodded a thank you as he watched his neighbor make his way down the path in the dark.

Bolting the door, Trevor gloated, "Better than expected."

He re-entered the bedroom. Kaitlyn lay semi-conscious on the bed, gazing up at him. Trevor sat down and pulled her into his arms.

"You were magnificent, darling." He combed a hand through her hair, stroking her gently.

Chapter 13

Pain

The pain in his leg yanked him from his dreams. Another sleepless night. Trevor climbed out of bed and searched for his pills. The light from the computer glowed dimly in the next room.

Trevor sat at the desk and pulled up his email. He scrolled through online dating sites he had previously signed up for.

All that seemed so juvenile now that he had Kaitlyn. None of the girls he had met online could even compare to his sweet pet. *She* was perfect.

A piece of paper slid silently from the desktop as Trevor moved the mouse to click on an important message in his inbox. His leg continued to throb as he read.

We regret to inform you that there are currently no matches on the donor list currently. We will continue to keep you informed of any changes.

Utah Medical Center

Dr. Croyle

Trevor squeezed his eyes shut as his own doctor's voice replayed in his head.

'It is estimated that without a bone marrow transplant, your life expectancy is approximately 10 to 20 months.'

Trevor closed the email, switched off the computer, and headed down to the kitchen. He couldn't think about that now. He had other things to dwell on.

He knew the chances of a bone marrow match in the data base were slim, on top of him being an only child and an orphan.

But Trevor was determined to succeed. He *had* to.

The crushed white powder swirled in his orange juice as he mixed the painkiller into his drink. The sharp pain in his leg had been growing significantly worse every day.

Trevor climbed back into bed and pulled Kaitlyn into his side tighter. She would save him, he smiled.

Dear Mom and Dad,

I was hoping to come out to visit you guys this weekend. Trevor has been begging to meet you guys. I will let you know for sure when we are coming. We are settled in here now and doing great.

Hope all is well, see you guys soon ~ Kait Manning

Kaitlin's mom read the email for a second time before calling her husband.

"Frank, you better come read this. It's Kait. She says she is gonna come visit us!"

Frank stepped up from behind Ellen.

"You don't say."

He scrunched his bushy eyebrows together and read the email over his wife's shoulder.

"Maybe she has finally come to her senses."

"Oh Frank. Don't start. She is bringing her husband home to meet us. This is progress. She's been *hiding* him from us this whole time. Now she's coming clean. Let's just accept that and go from here."

"Of course, she was hiding him from us! He's probably a drug addict or a welfare loafer. You know her type!"

"She is our *only* daughter. She married him, so we are stuck with her decision. She is being honest with us and brining him to meet us! It's nothing short of a miracle with the way you fly off the handle every time she looks at a boy. You scared off the last young man that even glanced her way. Hell, he left town because of you. No wonder she didn't want this one to meet us first. She's an adult. And so are you, so start *acting* like it."

Ellen stood and marched out of the room.

"It's your fault she moved away!" Ellen shouted from the other room.

Frank sighed, fearing his wife was right. His own daughter had lied and kept something so huge from them. He had noticed her distancing herself from them for a weeks before she moved out.

Perhaps, Frank wondered, *perhaps it was my fault.*

Frank made a silent promise to himself to give the boy a chance. *One chance...*

Chapter 14

RPM's

Trevor had picked up Kaitlyn's prescriptions from the local pharmacy and was just about to head back when Trevor spotted a familiar blond sporting dark shades strolling towards him.

"Hello, Tammy," he said, catching her eye.

Tammy immediately straightened herself.

"Well, lucky me. I was about to spoil myself buying needless lingerie. Perhaps I'll have lunch with you instead."

"Lunch and lingerie?" Trevor liked the pairing of the two. "Will there be room for dessert?"

Tammy giggled. "Have you been to the club yet?"

"I can't say that I have."

Tossing her blond hair over her shoulder, she guided Trevor toward her sporty yellow convertible parked nearby. She took the paper bag from Trevor and tossed it in the narrow bench seat in the rear and handed over her keys.

Trevor knew she was offering him more than just the opportunity to *drive* her sports car.

He accepted the keys and opened the passenger door for her. She slid into the warm black leather seats and let her short skirt slide up her thigh as she crossed her legs.

He shut the door and held her gaze for a moment. *Nothing subtle here,* he thought to himself as he rounded the back of the little car. Her eyes tracked his movements him from the rearview mirror.

The engine purred to life and Trevor imagined his passenger could have matched its RPM's.

Tammy slid her hand up Trevor's right thigh and then rested it on the black leather knob of the gear shift. He knew what she wanted to convey. *He may be driving, but she was still in control.* Trevor tried to hide his smile. She had no idea…

The road curved slightly as they rounded the lake and set out towards the hills. Each shift change seemed to excite her more.

He accelerated out of a turn and headed into a straightaway. Tammy slammed the car into 5th gear for him just as he engaged the clutch.

This was going to be fun.

The Club was a ritzy "members only" golf course with restaurant and bar. It conveniently offered 26 executive rooms in their boutique resort. The rolling manicured greens and perfectly placed pines framed the three-story colonial building.

Tammy insisted he valet the car at the front, and he obeyed. She interlocked her arm in his as they ascended the wide stone steps to the front entrance of the club.

As they neared the top, the doorman stepped out and held the door as they entered.

"Good morning, Mrs. Putten. I must say, you look ravishing as usual," the bellman complimented.

Tammy nodded and discreetly stuffed a folded-up bill into his vest pocket as she passed.

They were directed to a window seat overlooking the long stretch of grass of the ninth tee. The waiter approached and poured them each ice water in short wine glasses. Trevor could tell Tammy frequented this place as the roving staff all greeted her as they passed by.

Tammy smiled; her eyes poised on his.

Tammy was a distraction from his ultimate plan with Kaitlyn. He really didn't need this sidetrack. Tammy was literally offering herself to him with every gesture and toss of her hair.

This is too easy.

She was a liability, and he knew it. The more he played coy the more flagrant she became. He needed to shut it down, she could bring unwanted attention to him. Trevor lifted his right hand, signaling the waiter, who rushed back immediately.

"Bring us a bottle of champagne. Opus One, please."

Trevor knew she wanted *something* from him. What exactly, he hadn't figured out just yet. It puzzled him yet intrigued him all the same. Though her excessive flirting was becoming an irritation, he decided he wanted to solve the puzzle. Besides, she had no idea whom she was dealing with.

The young waiter returned with two flute glasses and a chilled bottle of bubbly wrapped in a white linen towel. He poured the carbonated liquid, bringing the foam to the brim without spilling a drop.

The waiter placed the bottle into an ice bucket stand next to the table and quietly departed.

Tammy gently caressed the condensation from the stem of her glass, holding Trevor's gaze.

Chapter 15

Good Girl

His watch read 3:23 pm. Trevor rolled out from under his blond bedfellow and tiptoed across the room. He hadn't planned on leaving Kaitlyn alone so long. He feared the sleeping pills would be wearing off already.

Trevor snatched up the phone from the desk and stepped into the bathroom to make a quick call, stretching the length of the cord to its max.

"Yes, this is Trevor Manning, room 21," he whispered into the phone. "Can you call me a taxi?"

Slipping from the room unnoticed, Trevor descended the stairs to the lobby. The bellman opened the door for Trevor as he approached.

"Come again," the bellman mused.

Trevor glanced back at the man with a knowing look.

The taxi ride back to town gave him a moment to think. His fling with Tammy had not been part of his plan, but something about her longed-for fulfillment. Whatever it was, he could feel her desperation. Trevor was drawn to desperation and need.

Desperation had been his driving force that pushed him to the edge of his soul, ultimately changing and making him who he had become. Desperation, left untreated, could become all consuming, robbing the very breath from your soul, if not treated appropriately.

As Trevor reached his car, he realized Kaitlyn's prescription had been left on that little leather bench in the backseat of Tammy's car.

"Damn it, Tammy...." he said, shaking his head.

Kaitlyn rubbed the sleep from her blurry eyes and curled into a ball on the bed. Suddenly she realized the lack of resistance as she pulled her legs to her chest.

She sat up and stared at her feet, no longer shackled. Her breath caught in her throat. Had he forgot to restrain her? Was this a test?

Kaitlyn rubbed her face as the residual effects of the drugs beckoned her to return to her pillow.

Slowing her breathing she listened for sounds of Trevor in the apartment. After a second of straining her ears, she quietly scooted off the bed.

Her bandaged feet padded across the floor to the sliding glass doors. The doors wouldn't open. The lock had been jammed.

Kaitlyn stood back wondering if she should break it or try for the front door.

She thought of her options. If she broke it and he *was* in the apartment, he would hear her and be on her in seconds.

I could scream to get the neighbors attention.

Jumping from a second story balcony might not be a good idea.

Or, she thought, *if he isn't in the apartment.... I could just walk straight out the front door to freedom.*

Swallowing her fear, she opted for the front door. Carefully easing down the stairs, she held her breath, listening for any indication that he had returned home.

As she rounded the corner, taking in the empty living room she felt a surge of excitement and anxiety.

This is it! I'm going to escape!

There, standing on bandaged feet, stood Kaitlyn at the bottom of the stairs. Trevor gripped the doorknob, positioning himself in the middle of the doorway.

"Hello darling, good to see you are up, but you really should stay off your feet until they have healed properly." Trevor slowly began to close the door.

Kaitlyn's heart pounded. She reminded herself that she had to be patient, *but the door is right there.*

Never mind that, Trevor is in her way. He was always in the way.

In one split second decision, Kaitlyn sprinted for the front door screaming, her arms flailing about.

"Help! Help!"

Trevor stepped forward and caught her small frame in his arms and lifted her off her feet.

He quickly put a hand over her mouth and carried her towards the living room. Kaitlyn tried to bite his hand and flung her heals into his shin as she tugged at the arm around her waist and mouth. Trevor squeezed her tighter, blocking oxygen from entering her nose or mouth.

Desperation took hold. She was so close, closer than *ever* before, only to be dragged back in once again. Kaitlyn could feel herself about to lose consciousness. The room began to darken.

"If you want to see your parents, I need to see some good behavior on your part."

He loosened his chokehold, enough for her to suck in gulps of air. Kaitlyn began sobbing under his hand. She continued to pull at his forearm trying to wrench herself free.

"I'll make you a deal. You and I can hang out downstairs, maybe even watch a movie together. I'll make us some dinner, open a bottle of wine. But you need to take your medicine and *chill out*. That means no fighting me, no screaming, and no running for the door, or else..."

His hand lowered from her mouth.

"Do we have a deal?"

Kaitlyn slowly looked up at her captor. His crystal blue eyes glistened beneath his stare. She nodded in agreement.

"Good!" he exclaimed, hopping to his feet. Kaitlyn found his sudden change in mood unsettling.

"I am really excited about seeing your parents next weekend," he went on.

Kaitlyn sat staring at the lake through the shear veil of the curtain. She wondered how far the drop was from her deck to the water. Not more than six feet she guessed, plus the railing.... maybe nine? She could survive that fall and likely be able to get up and run after impact depending on how deep the water was.

She could hear Trevor whistling cheerfully in the kitchen. Did he really plan to take her to her parents? She rolled her eyes and stared at the ceiling. He believed he was. Now it was up to her to play along until she could *tell* her parents or *anyone* who might listen, what was really going on. That this man was insane, a psychopath, and God knows what else.

Kaitlyn could feel her fists clenching and her wounds aching.

"Here is your medicine, love."

Kaitlyn took the dropper of tart liquid and reluctantly squeezed it into her mouth. Trevor smiled and marched back to the kitchen. When he turned, she spit as much of it out behind the pillow cushion as she could.

The doorbell rang. Kaitlyn wondered who that could possibly be. Trevor held a kitchen knife up in the air and pointed it at Kaitlyn, his eyes unflinching. Trevor opened the door slightly and peered out. Tammy leaned against the door jam and gazed up at him.

"You forgot something."

Glancing back at Kaitlyn, his eyes cold, knife extended in her direction.

"What's that?" he asked, returning his gaze to Tammy as he opened the door a little wider so she could peer in. Her eyes quickly darted to the interior, catching a glimpse of Kaitlyn on the couch.

"This really isn't a good time. My wife isn't well and she...."

Kaitlyn stood and screamed at the stranger at the door.

"Help!"

Trevor eased the door nearly shut, poking his head out for Tammy.

"See," he said, rolling his eyes. "Today isn't one of her good days."

"She *is* crazy!" Tammy found herself saying.

"No, no, no. She is just confused. She has had a really tough time."

Kaitlyn scrambled to her feet, shuffling towards the door. "Help me! He's trapped me here!" she screamed.

"Oh, my goodness. I..... I am so sorry. I just wanted to bring you the prescription you left in..... my car," she said, keeping her voice low.

Trevor waved the knife at Kaitlyn as she approached the door.

"Help! Save me! Call the police!" Kaitlyn screamed as she came within six feet of the front door. "Please! He kidnapped me!"

Trevor kept himself composed and affectionately brushed Tammy's cheek with the back of his hand.

"Thank you," he said, taking the package. "Thank you for everything."

He closed the door and engaged the dead bolt with a slam.

Leaning against the door, Trevor stared down at the knife in his hand, sensually running his fingers up and down the side of the blade as he spoke.

"I thought we had a deal."

He stepped forward and met her eyes once more.

"How can I trust you now?"

Kaitlyn shook her head as fresh tears began to fall.

"Now I'll *have* to punish you." Trevor pouted in a show of regret.

Kaitlyn backed up towards the couch. "No, don't. Please."

He snatched up her arm and with one swift slice, a short red line appeared across her right wrist, and then another.

Red oozing slices crisscrossed her forearm as blood trickled down her arm pooling in the palm of her hand.

Trevor tightened his grip on Kaitlyn's wrist until she screamed in agony. He slapped her across the face.

"Quiet," he ordered, "or I'll slit your throat too."

Kaitlyn swallowed back her cries and tried to focus on the knife. His threats and the sight of her own blood streaming down her arm sunk the threat of his words deep into her soul.

For a moment, Kaitlyn saw death as her only way out. It would put an end to the torment. No, she asserted to herself. *He* needed to be punished. He had to die. She vowed to survive long enough to see it.

Kaitlyn's head felt light. Trevor guided her to the kitchen sink letting her blood escape into the drain.

"You need to do something for me," he stated flatly. "It requires you being a very, *very* good girl. I am not sure you are capable of that."

Her head began to spin.

She stared at the blood swirling down the drain until they landed on an object of interest. There, within reach, quietly laid the kitchen knife.

Her left hand inched closer to it. She envisioned grasping the handle and shoving it deep into his chest, watching him fall to the floor as he bled to his end.

The tips of her fingers slowly slid toward the kitchen knife, taking a sharp inhale as she reached for it, but she was too late.

Trevor wrenched her body around to face him. He pinned her up against the counter as he pressed a clean towel around her arm.

For a moment he just stared deep into her eyes. His were a cold steel blue, unflinching, uncaring.

"Hungry?" he asked, returning to the Trevor she hated most. Without a word, he lifted Kaitlyn by the hips and placed her on the countertop. "You stay there."

His right hand picked up the kitchen knife from the counter and brought it in front of her, close to Kaitlyn's neck. He turned it over, admiring the steel. Flipping on the hot water, he began washing the blade with soap, turning it over and over in his hand under the water.

Kaitlyn watched in silence as he returned to his meal prepping.

"Open this," he said, handing her a can of tomato paste and an opener.

Kaitlyn envisioned breaking his skull open with the can as she turned the tin top in her hands. She removed the lid and handed the can to Trevor.

He took it, watching her as he stirred the paste into his pan. He added chopped onions and garlic in a sizzle of aroma.

"Taste it."

He raised a spoonful to her mouth.

Kaitlyn reluctantly tasted it. She feigned a smile and nodded at him.

Trevor kissed her on the cheek.

"How's the bleeding?"

Kaitlyn glanced at her arm wrapped in a towel. She had almost forgotten her wound, distracted with ideas of injuring him.

She let her body go limp as he moved her from the kitchen counter. He guided her to the table where she sat quietly waiting for his next mood change.

As she chewed, she imagined smashing her wine glass against the wall and stabbing him with the broken stem. She wondered if she was going crazy. Never had she imagined inflicting violence upon someone. Trevor was turning her into someone she didn't want to be.

She thought about the times he held her down, made her helpless, made her beg, and the smile he'd give her. Oh, she hated that smile. She intended to do the same to him, hurt him and then smile, just once. Once would be enough.

He wanted to watch TV together. Even after her attempts to escape, Trevor did not modify his plans for the evening. They were exactly where he had imagined they'd be at this point in the night. For the first time, she found herself wishing she could just go back to bed. Kaitlyn silently prayed that she could keep her composure until then.

Trevor peeled his eyes away from the TV.

"I'm gonna push our visit to your parents back a week or two. I am not convinced you are ready."

Kaitlyn listened. The night was still not over.

"I can't trust that you won't harm yourself," he said, pointing to her wounds.

A coldness washed over Kaitlyn as she tried to understand him. He was trying to convince her, or perhaps himself, that *she* was responsible for her injuries.

Desperation gripped her throat like the cold boney fingers of death.

"I want you to talk to Dr. Putten again. I think you need more help."

"Talk about what?" she asked.

"About how you are forgetful, and troubled, and sometimes hurt yourself."

Kaitlyn stared blankly at the TV, knowing full well there was nothing she could do to change his mind or his made-up stories.

Trevor tilted his head.

"Perhaps we *are* getting somewhere. I'll call him now."

Trevor lifted the phone to her ear as it rang on the other line.

"Be a good girl," he whispered.

She vaguely remembered the doctor's last visit. She felt a growing unease knowing that if she were to scream for help again, she'd only be giving more truth to Trevor's story.

"Hello?" the man's voice answered. "Dr. Putten here......hello?"

Trevor placed his right hand over her throat and gently squeezed. Kaitlyn gripped his wrist.

"Yes. Doctor... Uhm. Doctor..."

"Putten," Trevor coaxed in her ear, his breath warm on her neck as he held her tight.

"Dr. Putten?"

"Yes. Who is this?"

"Kaitlyn..." She felt her heart thundering in her chest as she struggled with the words. "This is Kaitlyn."

"Manning," Trevor added, gently laying a kiss on ear.

"This is Kaitlyn *Manning*. I need help."

"Hello Kait. Thank you for calling me. What can I do for you?"

Paralyzed, she shook her head and handed the phone back to Trevor.

"Hey, it's me."

Trevor interjected as he squeezed Kaitlyn tighter against his chest. He ran a hand through her hair and tugged slightly.

"Yeah, she had a pretty bad day, but I convinced her to call you. I don't know if it's a bad time or...."

"No, it's fine. I'm surprised she called me. She is lucid right now. Should I come over?"

Suddenly Trevor felt unprepared for a visit.

"No, no. That's ok. I just felt it would be good for *her* to ask you for help herself instead of me trying to push it on her." Trevor turned to her, smiling. "It needs to be her idea."

"Of course. I'm glad she called. Put me back on the phone with her and I'll see what I can do."

"Thank you."

Trevor handed Kaitlyn the phone and returned his hand to her throat. He caressed it lightly as she listened to Dr. Putten's advice. Not knowing what was being said on the other line, he watched and monitored Kaitlyn's response. She was, after all, being a *good girl*.

After several minutes of a nearly one-sided conversation, Kaitlyn thanked him and hung up the phone.

"What did he say?" Trevor asked, curious.

"He said he is gonna help me try to feel happy again…"

"Aww, you know I am the *only* one who can do that."

Kaitlyn stared at the floor envisioning his lifeless body lying before her, the apartment floor awash with a pool of *his* blood, and the knife resting in her hands.

Yes, she thought, *he is the only one who can make me happy.*

<u>Chapter 16</u>

Miss Me

A brief email informed Kaitlyn's parents that their visit would have to be pushed back due to Trevor's work, and that they would be in touch soon.

A week passed with Kaitlyn getting used to the routine of being chained to the wall during the day while Trevor was gone at work. A short release when he came home for lunch, sometimes hungry for more than food, then replacing her tethers until he returned at 4 pm, where he would make a show of dinner and snuggling on the couch until she fell asleep in his arms.

She had the most freedom in the evening when he would have her help cook dinner, the knives all but missing from the kitchen.

His growing desire for control developed a need for Kaitlyn to greet him on her knees, head down and eyes on the floor. She would tell him she had been a good girl while he was out.

Then she could supplicate for food, drinks, and other privileges.

Kaitlyn felt numb inside. The drugs he fed her helped dull her senses. His touch, his breath, his voice - all part of a foggy dream she tried to ignore. As much as she felt disconnected, she never gave up hope for an escape.

Trevor was careful, never letting her out of his sight or near any utensils that she could potentially harm him or herself with.

This is my new life. She relented. *At least I'm alive.*

"Kaity, I'm home," Trevor called from downstairs.

Kaitlyn had lost track of time fantasizing Trevor's demise.

He raced up the stairs.

"I have good news!" he said, stepping into the bedroom. "I just got promoted. Do you know what that means?" He plopped himself down on the bed, reaching for her restraints. "It means we should celebrate."

Kaitlyn scrambled to the floor feeling guilty for not being prepared and kneeling at his feet.

"Did you miss me?"

He lowered his face next to hers, his lips brushing her cheeks. She bowed her head.

As much loathing as Kaitlyn felt for her captor, she wondered if she was being presented with an *opportunity*.

He unlatched her tethers and scooped her up as he regularly did when he returned on his lunch break. He carried her down the stairs and placed her at the table as he happily hummed to himself in the kitchen.

"Trevor?" she said aloud. She had to know. "Do you think we will still be able to visit my parents?"

The utensil in Trevor's hand fell on the countertop, ringing through the kitchen. Trevor stood still; his humming ceased.

Too soon? She wondered, biting her lip.

Easing himself around the kitchen corner post, he looked at Kaitlyn with cold, calculating eyes.

She lowered her gaze, feeling as though she stepped out of her bounds.

"That is a great idea," he said. "Let's go next weekend."

Kaitlyn was simultaneously relieved and disappointed, counting the added days she would have to comply with her captor's delusions until she could finally see her parents.

She forced a thankful smile.

Trevor talked of his various client encounters at work as he munched on his turkey sandwich. Kaitlyn pretended to listen.

She imagined her turkey meat hardening until it became a weapon. A sharp one.

Where should I stab him this time? The thought filled her with unexpected energy.

"Baby?" he had been saying something, though she couldn't recall what.

She rubbed her face as if tired. It was easy to get away with feigning drowsiness.

"Sorry, what was that?" She groggily rubbed her eyes. "What did you say, hon?"

The added sentiment of affection distracted Trevor.

"You must be tired. Let's finish our sandwiches and then I'll take you back upstairs. We can cuddle a bit before I go back to work."

"I'd like that," she lied.

As they quietly lay in each other's arms, Kaitlyn contemplated more ways to convince Trevor to trust her.

"I think my parents are going to love you."

Trevor bolted upright. "Really?"

Kaitlyn brushed the side of his face, staring him dead in the eye.

"They just have to know you the way I do."

Trevor kissed her on the lips, and, as he withdrew, he whispered, "I love you."

A deep sadness struck Kaitlyn in her heart. As messed up as this man was, he *believed* every lie he told her, told himself.

She wondered if he would truly believe hers.

She feigned embarrassment and disbelief, knowing he would eat up her humility. She would get what she wanted. He would grant her an actual trip to her parents, perhaps even sooner.

"Maybe..." she paused. "Maybe I could cook dinner for *you* tonight?" She held her breath. "I have a special dish I'd like to make. I could make it for you, in celebration of your promotion?"

Trevor raised up on his elbow and leaned over Kaitlyn. "I would love that."

His delight nearly levitated him from the bed as he stood and straightened his clothes. He quickly washed his hands in the bathroom and ran them through his hair.

She stared at him for a moment and wondered how a man, such a charming man, could end up like this.

Trevor loomed over her, looking down at his prey.

Soon, he thought to himself, *soon. She was coming around. Everything was falling into place.*

He slowly replaced the restraints on Kaitlyn and held her gaze.

"I'll be back soon."

He reached for her neck, firmly holding it before lightly glided down her chest.

"Miss me."

Kaitlyn knew she had no choice. She inhaled, restraining her desire to pull away. She glanced up at his eyes as he fondled her left breast. Locking away the resentment she harbored towards him, she nodded. She would miss him. She would have to continue to miss him. But not for long, she thought to herself.

Chapter 17

The Lie

Trevor locked the front door of the apartment, his newly installed, key-only deadbolt, which seemed to comfort him as he walked to the car. He tried to ignore the throbbing in his pants. He couldn't think about that now.

Trevor imagined her body sprawled out across the bed as he drove. Trevor inhaled, feeling short of breath as he realized he was stopped at a green light.

"Why does she have to get under my skin like she does?" he asked himself aloud as he drove.

The rest of the day he caught his mind returning to the image of Kaitlyn on her stomach as his hands moved over her body.

He massaged his client in the dark wishing it was her he was touching instead of the 56-year-old whiplash victim on his table. The dim lighting in his treatment room offered him the anonymity he desired, letting his hands take the lead.

Crushing handfuls of hair between his palms he grinded his fingers into his client's scalp.

Trevor caught himself chuckling out loud as he thought of how fiery she had been that first night. Even kicking him in the jaw hadn't slowed him down, but only excited him more.

She was a fighter and he liked that, yet... he released the final strands of hair from his patient and dove his thumbs into the side of her neck, letting them glide up to the base of her skull over the thin layer of warm oil.

She was tenacious, he thought. He loved that unbreakable determination. She seemed to be coming around, he reminded himself. She stopped trying to escape. She even missed him.

Is she *playing* me? *Is her new affection a lie?*

Of course, it is, he thought.

She had the spirit of a wild horse since day one. There was no way he had tamed her in just six weeks.

Trevor's cheeks flushed with anger. He had believed her for a moment. That alone made him angry at himself as much as her. A smile formed at the corner of his mouth. Of course. She was going to play the good girl like he asked, hoping to gain enough freedom that she might escape and ruin all his plans.

Though he admired her strong will, he knew he needed to punish her for fooling him so.

Trevor had a thought. *I will just let her play this pretend game.*

He had to admit he liked it. He liked knowing she was playing. That made it so much more exciting.

Sure, she posed more of a threat this time around. *But*, he reasoned, *no harm in having a bit of fun.*

Kaitlyn stared out the window, several scenarios of escape unfolding in her mind, one by one.

No one is looking for me, she finally admitted to herself. *Not even my parents, at least not for a while.*

She had left them under strained circumstances. After all, she had intended to get as far away from them as possible.

The thought of her parents sent an un-wielding ache in her stomach. The pain turned to acid as it crept up her throat, threatening to launch at one more desperate thought.

Kaitlyn dashed to the bathroom and threw up her lunch in the toilet.

Inhaling slowly, she calmed herself down.

After a month... yes. Why hadn't they insisted on hearing from me. Didn't they want to make sure I was okay, eating, breathing...oh god...wouldn't they?

The acid returned as she questioned her now strained relationship with her parents.

They had offered her help when they thought she needed it, yet she had bluntly refused. The last thing she thought she wanted was her parents judging her and her decisions. Now all she could think about was how much she wanted them.

She would endure any scrutiny if she could just be under their care again. Guilt from years of resentment crept into her stomach making it roll once more.

Suddenly she realized Trevor had to have contacted them. Or

else why would he even mention visiting them?

"Oh, no!"

Kaitlyn felt a wave of heat rush up her spine.

"Have they been convinced of this charade? Will they even believe me if I tell them?"

She felt the knot in her stomach grow, twisting and squeezing until the hurt was nearly unbearable. She moaned uncontrollably.

What did he say to them? What has he done?

She returned to the bed, exhausted. The glassy grey water rippled slightly as two swans nuzzled each other between the reeds against the bank.

The calmness of the water was her only solace.

She imagined herself as one of the ducks that glided effortlessly across the lake. She closed her eyes and let the image lift her from her chains, soaring over the lake on wings of gold. The clouds above beckoned her higher and higher.

Drugs, she thought. *It's just the drugs.* White cotton clouds surrounded her from all sides as she dozed off to sleep.

Chapter 18

Cheers

Portabella mushrooms with feta crumbled over the tops, sautéed onions, crème sauce and a side of green salad. Kaitlyn stood in the kitchen peering over her culinary creation, spatula in hand.

A thin blue button-down shirt of Trevor's hung loosely over her as she moved about the kitchen. Trevor sipped his Pinot Noir while he leaned against the kitchen wall.

"You know your way around the kitchen."

He enjoyed her efforts to impress him. Such a performance, he thought to himself.

A test was in order. She had talked to Dr. Putten on the phone twice in the last week. She had made a good show of her attempt at progress and self-control. Dr. Putten's diagnosis was solid, believing the medication he had prescribed seemingly doing the trick.

Placing his wine glass on the counter, Trevor slowly moved closer. Gently resting his palms over her shoulders, he eased his body against hers, softly pinning her to the counter. She inhaled sharply but didn't try to move away.

He let his lips brush her neck, his breath cascading her hair from her face. He tried to gauge just how far she might play along.

Kaitlyn's hands refused to continue their duties; her body suddenly rigid.

She turned to him, forcing a smile at the monster

"Let's eat," she urged, as she wedged a plate between them.

"Smells good."

They moved to the small dining table and sat across from each other as they ate.

"I like the new you." Trevor coaxed.

He stretched his hand across the table and gathered hers. His thumb brushed over the thin wedding ring on her hand. He wondered how far he could manipulate her.

Trevor filled his wine glass again and then hers.

"Cheers," he said, urging her to drink. "To moving forward, *together.*"

Kaitlyn swallowed the cobwebs in her throat.

"Cheers," she said, barely audible. Her glass clinked his and they both drank.

"I can't take it anymore," Trevor said.

Kaitlyn was struck by the lust in Trevor's stare. He stood and held out his hand. Reluctantly, she gave him hers and he guided to the bedroom.

She tried to distract him.

"Don't you want desert…" she paused.

Trevor's eyes burned with desire.

"Of course, I do."

Kaitlyn held her breath, searching her mind for other ways to stall him. She was playing along, but that didn't mean things had to go the way he wanted them to.

"Actually, I was going to ask you for something."

Tilting his head, he waited for her request. "Anything," he lied.

"Do you think you could open another bottle of wine?"

"After," he whispered, pulling her into his arms.

Her shoulders slumped, realizing she would lose either way, just as she had all those other nights.

"But I thought we were celebrating?" she asked coyly. Putting her good girl face on as she followed him into the bedroom.

"Okay," he sighed. "But I want you in a silk nighty when I return.

Kaitlyn nodded, her entire body screaming from the inside out.

This is her test, Trevor said to himself as he jogged down the stairs for another bottle of wine.

Trevor placed two glasses on the counter. Then, pulling out his freshly powdered love cocktail, dosed Kaitlyn's drink. A tiny slice of his self image had been carved away every time he resorted to drugging his girl. There were dozens of women he could have willingly, though, none of them compared to his Kait.

Just for good measure, Trevor made sure the front door, and deck doors were securely locked.

As he ascended the stairs, he pictured Kaitlyn trying to unlock the deck door, or perhaps hiding behind the door with the lamp ready to smash into his head.

Instead, Kaitlyn lay on her side on top of the bed spread, wearing her lavender night gown.

Excellent, he thought as he handed her the spiked drink.

Kaitlyn took the glass and placed it to her lips taking a small sip, eyes on Trevor.

"Thank you," she said getting to her feet. "You really do treat me well. I'm sorry I didn't realize it until now,"

Kaitlyn took his wine glass and placed it on the dresser behind him.

She kissed his cheek and wrapped her arms around him, leaning her head on his chest. Trevor inhaled the scent of her hair, pulling her tighter, closer.

Kaitlyn quietly switched glasses before pulling away, guiding him to the bed.

"Cheers," she said holding her glass in the air. "To your new job and promotion!"

"Cheers."

Kaitlyn took a long sip of wine, watching as he did the same. She pulled back the covers of the bed and slid into the cool crisp sheets and plunged her feet under the blanket.

Trevor waited, watching her as he took another sip of wine. She seemed eager to *prove herself* to him, he thought.

Trevor clasped a restraint on one of her ankles, flipped off the light and climbed in next to her, pulling her under him as his lips found hers.

She felt hollow inside realizing that even if the drugs affected him, she would still be shackled to the bed.

Kaitlyn sighed a breath of relief as she pushed Trevor's unconscious body off hers.

One small victory she thought as she let her head drop to her pillow.

Chapter 19

Pretending

The doorbell rang.

Trevor shot his eyes open and glanced at the time. 9:30 am.

He rolled out of bed and pulled on a pair of gray sweats. He rubbed his blurry eyes with numb hands and stumbled down the stairs.

Kaitlyn was left alone. Un-drugged and conscious. She sprang from the bed, her heart racing as she glanced around the room.

This is my chance, she thought to herself, as she searched for the key to her restraints.

Her name was being called from below. Oh god. Trevor's footsteps were approaching the stairs already. Paralyzed, she stood in the center of the bedroom. She could hear her inner voice screaming for her to move, scream...anything! But her body went cold. Losing this chance didn't terrify her, not nearly enough as the thought of never having another.

"Kaity?" Trevor peeked his head into the room. "Get dressed. We've got company."

Dressed? She glanced at the dresser and the closet doors, somewhat lost. Trevor crossed the room and gathered up a pair of thin leggings and a light blue tank top for her. She dressed as he watched, all the while wondering who or what was waiting for her downstairs.

She followed Trevor down the stairs to find Dr. Putten sitting in the living room. Inhaling sharply, her eyes glanced from Trevor to the doctor. She had been severely drugged and out of her mind the last time she saw Dr. Putten in person.

Guiding Kaitlyn to the sofa, they sat across from Dr. Putten.

Trevor's touch was gentle yet possessive. Kaitlyn gritted her teeth as she sat with his arm around her, strong and unmoving.

"I'm sorry I'm late," Dr. Putten began, "I had a situation at the office. Anyway, I didn't want to miss our meeting and instead of calling I thought an in-person visit would be better."

Waiving a hand, "Honestly, we forgot," his expression sheepish, "Last night was, uh ... one of our better nights and I guess we slept in."

"Good to hear. Well, Kait, tell me how you are feeling today?"

Suddenly put on the spot, she didn't know what to say.

Do I try to convince this man of the truth and risk all the work I have done to fool Trevor so far, or continue to play along?

When she didn't answer right away, Dr. Putten decided to

recap.

"Let's see. You have experienced some memory loss at times, with confusion as to who you are, who your husband is..."

Kaitlyn felt her teeth grinding as he recounted the lies, he had been fed.

"And at times some violent outbursts, with the occasional self-harm," he added.

That about sums me up, Kaitlyn thought, refraining from rolling her eyes.

"I have been feeling much better. Thank you," she stated graciously. "And Trevor has been really patient with me," she said, squeezing his arm.

Trevor found himself oddly turned amused.

"Yes, and she made me dinner, and we made love like it was the first time," he added.

Kaitlyn wondered if he remembered anything from the night

before. No, she assured herself.

She acknowledged that the anti-depressants he had prescribed were working and that she felt better. She knew she had to, otherwise Dr. Putten would prescribe more drugs, which was the last thing Kaitlyn needed.

Dr. Putten nodded slowly.

"Good to hear that, but these things take time. We need to get to the root of the issue. And a simple pill isn't going to *fix* anything just like that."

Kaitlyn realized coldly that no matter what she said, she'd only let Trevor win.

"I have an admittance referral form here. I want you to take it and consider it carefully."

Trevor accepted the form with a display of regret.

"Kait, why don't you go upstairs and let the doctor and I talk for a while."

Kaitlyn stood on trembling knees; the lies had begun to pile up in her mind. She wanted to scream at Dr. Putten! *It's all just façade; an act, perhaps the greatest performance of my life!*

She swallowed back the lump growing in her throat her mind lost in a trance as she quietly ascended the stairs.

"Look, Roger..."

"I know what you are going to say, Trevor. But she needs *professional* help. More than I can give, and more than you can do. She needs 24/7 care by professionals, in a facility equipped to handle her. I know you want to take care of her yourself, and that's honorable, but you are doing too much and it's taking its toll on you. From what I see, she is going through the motions in hopes of *seeming* better and improved, but honestly, this is just one more indication that she is getting worse."

Trevor let his head fall into his hands. "How did you know? How did you know she was just.... *pretending* to be better?" he sighed. "I admit, I love the almost-normal Kait, but... she really isn't stable. I can barely get home from work in time to keep her safe from herself."

Roger put a hand on Trevor's shoulder. "I know, but she can only keep this act up for period, then she will snap. You don't want that. She could really hurt herself and perhaps even you in the process. Promise me you will consider this. It doesn't have to be permanent. But it is what she *needs*."

"I will." Trevor felt proud as his plan began to fall into place. "I just want to take her to visit her parents first. I haven't even met them yet. They really should have a chance to be part of this decision."

"You are a good man." Dr. Putten rose to his feet. "Take some time and let me know if *you* need anything. Be safe," he said as he exited the apartment.

Trevor sat in the living room with the paperwork in his hands. It was exactly what he wanted, though earlier than he expected.

The floor upstairs creaked above him.

"Kaity? Come."

A second later Kaitlyn peaked around the stairwell, waiting for instruction.

He couldn't help but smile. Perhaps she *was* ready to visit her parents.

"You know what this is, don't you?" He held the paper in front of her. "It's an *order* for you to seek some serios professional help. It would mean you would be in a hospital, away from me," he sighed. "Is that what you want?"

The question paralyzed her. She felt the walls closing in.

He would have me committed? Why? She couldn't fathom a

reason. She wondered if his question was another test.

"I want to stay with you," she lied.

It was what he wanted to hear, though as she said the words aloud, she suddenly saw the appeal of being in a mental hospital, far away from him.

She would be free of him, free to tell her story to those who would listen. Free.

But who would believe a crazy person? She worried.

"Tell you what." He ran his fingers through her hair. "When we see your parents next weekend, you will tell them. And I mean tell them *everything*. How you hurt yourself, how I am always here to help you and keep you from hurting yourself. And... how you have been so confused lately, forgetting who I am, and how much you love me."

The words cut at her like the kitchen knife that sliced her wrist. Could she tell her parents such things?

What would they even think? Who would they believe?

"I will be with you the whole time to support you. I love you, Kaity. I really don't want you to be away from me. Not yet anyway."

Kaitlyn swallowed. There it was.

"Perhaps we can talk to your parents about the help you need. And together we can work out a treatment plan."

Kaitlyn nodded and let her head fall on Trevor's chest. Everything had become surreal. She could pretend she was snuggling her lover, in a happy relationship, in her new apartment in her new sweet little town on the lake. But it was only pretend, only an act as she waited for the right opportunity to escape.

Escape! Yes.

She would hold on to that thought, that exhilarating feeling. But for now, she would be forced to live in his pretend life.

Chapter 20

Perfect

Kaitlyn lifted a light pink sweater from her dresser and placed it on the bed next to the suitcase. Trevor chatted about a client he thought was interesting as he shaved in the bathroom mirror.

Kaitlyn gave a dutiful nod as she half listened.

"Grab my blue button up shirt, will you hon?" Trevor asked from the bathroom.

Kaitlyn opened the closet doors and scanned the section her captor had adopted as his own. She knew which one. It was his favorite. Or was it her *least* favorite? She couldn't tell.

Her reasoning had become foggy.

Pulling it from its hanger, she watched her fingers grip a button and tear it from its stitching.

That felt good.

"I think it's missing a button," she called as she tossed the thin white plastic button to the back of the closet.

Trevor stepped into the doorway with a quizzical look on his freshly shaven face.

"Really?" He rubbed his bare chest as he moved closer to examine the shirt in Kaitlyn's hand.

Kaitlyn glanced at the floor feeling a tear form in her left eye.

I can get through this. I will see my parents tonight.

She had been a *good girl* for so long to get to this day. She couldn't mess it up now. She was so close.

Trevor lifted her chin as he moved closer.

"Are you okay?" he asked.

Squashing any trace of emotion, gazed out the window. "I'm fine,"

The lake, it was her solace. She had chosen this very apartment because of its view, telling herself she would wake up every morning and see that lake, feeling blessed to live a long and happy life here. Now she looked at that lake every morning for strength to carry on. To make it just one more day.

"I don't think so," he said, suspicious. He pulled her down to the bed next to him. "Are you scared to see your parents?"

"No..."

She wasn't even sure anymore.

"Those don't look like tears of joy. Tell me what is upsetting you."

You mean on top of me being a prisoner in this absurd fantasy of yours? She wanted to say, the words on the tip of her tongue.

"I am worried my parents will be upset with me," she admitted.

"Why?"

You, for one.

"I haven't spoken to them since I left."

"Don't worry about that. I have kept them updated on your condition."

Not everything. Not yet.

She nodded and returned to rummaging through drawers and

refolding clothes, desperate to distract Trevor from her anxiety.

"Kait," Trevor called, his voice was sharp and commanding.

Startled, she turned to face him.

"I expect no less than perfect behavior from you."

Kaitlyn nodded with a forced smile. "Of course."

"That's my girl," he said, pulling her into his arms.

He kissed her softly on the lips and then again more passionately.

"You have nothing to fear. I won't let anything bad happen."

But I will.

Chapter 21

The Accident

Kaitlyn followed Trevor to her car. He opened the passenger side and guided her in. She was surprised when he produced a shiny pair of handcuffs for her to put on. Without a word of protest, she held out her wrists.

He casually engaged the child lock before closing her door. How thoughtful, Kaitlyn mused.

Pulling away from her lakefront condo, Kaitlyn glanced back at her prison. What she had intended to be her fresh start, her sanctuary, now a place of dread and terror.

Her chest tightened at the thought of never seeing inside that bedroom again.

He had insisted she take his special tincture before the drive. Knowing that fighting him would be useless, she took the tincture and waited for the effects to take hold.

Kaitlyn felt her eyelids grow heavy. She had grown accustomed to the drowsiness. She leaned her head against the cool glass of the window, and let her eyes shut, listening to the rhythm of the highway.

Trevor stole a glance at his sleeping angel beside him. The drugs had lulled her to sleep. Trevor returned his eyes to the road just in time to see a truck, pulling a long horse trailer, swerve violently into Trevor's lane.

Trevor slammed on the breaks! The two vehicles skidded

sideways as they hurled down the black top toward each other.

Kaitlyn screamed, awaking to the oncoming vehicle in their lane. The two vehicles collided. The horse trailer was wrenched from its hitch and toppled onto its side, sliding toward the shoulder of the oncoming lane.

Tires squealed, glass shattered, metal twisted, and screams filled the air.

Suddenly, everything was silent.

Kaitlyn was no longer a prisoner.

Trevor was no longer working on his plan.

Trevor rubbed his shoulder where the seatbelt had wrenched his body during the impact.

A loud cry from the other vehicle broke the stunned silence.

"Kaitlyn!" Trevor shouted.

Finally, Kaitlyn blinked her eyes. A trickle of blood emerged from her from her right temple.

"Tell me where it hurts."

"Everything," Kaitlyn answered, her head spinning.

"Be more specific," Trevor demanded.

"I think I'm okay," Kaitlyn groaned, holding her head. "I just... hit my head."

Running his hands over her shoulders, down her arms and legs, he scanned for other injuries. He then examined Kaitlyn's head and her wound above her right eye.

"You'll be okay." He sighed with genuine relief.

He unbuckled his seatbelt and crawled through the broken window, ignoring his bloodied left arm from the glass. He rounded the mangled vehicle and pulled at Kaitlyn's door until it gave. He tugged at her seat belt, but it wouldn't unlatch. He could hear multiple cries of distress from the other vehicle as he fought the restraint.

"Son of a..." he growled.

Trevor marched to the trunk and kicked it several times until it opened. Finding the first aid kit, he snatched up the small scissors. Sawing at thick material, he struggled to pull Kaitlyn from the belt.

Trevor felt the surge of adrenaline coursing through his veins as he scanned the onlookers for anyone of authority.

He quickly dug into his pockets for the small key to the handcuffs. Unlocking her wrists, he slid the coughs under the seat and guided Kaitlyn out of the car.

The highway bordered a steep sloping bank covered in pebbles and tufts of thin yellow grass.

Trevor gestured toward an incline off the highway.

"I'm gonna see if the people in the truck need help." Trevor pointed at her with the small scissors in his hand, "Don't be stupid, Kait. I'm trusting you."

Kaitlyn scrambled up the bank and waited. She watched Trevor jog across the highway to the wrecked truck and trailer.

"Call for help!"

Kaitlyn turned to see a woman approaching. She stumbled up the bank and knelt on the turf next to her.

"Here, call for help." Out of breath the lady handed Kaitlyn a cell phone.

"Help?" Kaitlyn paused. "The police!" Her head throbbed and

her fingers suddenly felt foreign as she fumbled with the phone.

She pressed the numbers 9-1-1 and listened as the line began to ring. Kaitlyn's eyes tracked across the road to overturned trailer. Someone or something screamed from inside.

Trevor glanced back at her, his stare sharp and calculating. He could clearly see she had a phone in her hand.

A voice came on the line.

"9-1-1, what's your emergency?"

"I need help! We were in an accident."

"What's your location?"

Kaitlyn watched Trevor as he moved to the overturned truck.

"Mile 132, out bound lane. I am not exactly sure what happened, but we hit a truck."

"Is anyone injured?"

"Yes..." Kaitlyn whispered, making sure Trevor was preoccupied. "I am. I need help. I have been kidnapped. Please help me. The man I am with is a monster. I need help. Please send someone to help me." Kaitlyn began sobbing between her words as she tried to tell the operator everything.

"Ma'am, an officer will be with you as soon as possible. Please remain calm--"

The line went dead.

"Hello?"

Kaitlyn searched the screen on the phone, but the battery had suddenly died. She felt herself groan with anxiety.

Why couldn't I have just called my parents?

She tried to assure herself that it wouldn't matter. Help was coming. *They will believe me. They must!*

Trevor returned to the car and collected the handcuffs, then wrapped them in a towel and shoved them and the cell phone under the spare tire compartment of the trunk.

Once his secret was safe, he jogged over to the other vehicle and helped an older gentleman lift his bruised wife out of the truck.

She was shaking and holding her arm. The older gentleman's face and elbow were covered in blood.

"What's your name, ma'am?" Trevor asked.

"Nancy."

"Tell me what hurts."

Trevor's' paramedic experience kicked in, his voice calm and reassuring. As much as he wanted to focus on his plan and keep Kaitlyn quiet, he had to maintain composure. The police would be here soon. There was no telling what Kaitlyn had said to them on the phone. Appearing to be the hero, as usual, would only help offset any negative shadow Kaitlyn might try to cast.

Trevor ran his hands along the woman's limbs and asked all the appropriate questions.

"I…I don't know," she stammered.

"Let's get you off the road."

The woman winced as she tried to take a step.

"It's ok, I got you." Trevor offered as he scooped up the older woman and carried her across the highway, safely depositing her next to Kaitlyn and the onlooker.

"Did you call 911?" he asked.

Kaitlyn nodded. He held her gaze for a moment and then swiftly took the phone from her.

Trevor marched back toward the wreckage. The old man frantically shuffled around the truck waving at Trevor for help. Suddenly, Trevor realized what the constant screaming sound had been – a horse. An injured horse. Trevor scrambled up the side of the overturned trailer and looked down.

"Please," the old man cried. "Help her."

Trevor nodded and reached out his had to assist the man in climbing up to the side of the trailer.

Together the two men pried the side door open and peered down. One horse lay motionless, the other wailing for help. Fear consumed its wide black eyes as it gasped for air and kicked at the air.

The older gentleman jumped down into the trailer and stood over the beast.

"There's nothing you can do," Trevor warned. "It has two broken legs and a chunk of metal in its gut.

"No, no, no…" the old man said.

Trevor looked back at Kaitlyn watching from the bank.

He hopped into the trailer and stood over the injured animal.

Traffic had begun to congest around the scene, horns blaring, and people emerged from their cars to gawk at the accident.

"No, I can't do it," the old man sobbed to Trevor.

Trevor sighed and moved toward the animal. He took in the horse's terrified eyes, and for a moment they understood each other.

The old man sobbed into his hands at the feet of his horse.

"I can't do it." He said handing Trevor a forty-five-caliber pistol. "Please, just make her pain stop. I can't bare for her to suffer."

Trevor understood. He took the pistol and aimed between the horses' wide frightened eyes.

BANG!

Kaitlyn gasped as she wrapped her arms around the woman's

shoulders. Feeling numb to the scene, she held the woman next to her mourning the loss of her dear animals.

Sirens echoed in the distance.

Kaitlyn pulled the older woman into her arms and let her cry on her shoulder.

Trevor gently stroked the horses face and the life slowly departed from its eyes.

Trevor attempted several times to assist the man out of the trailer, but eventually gave up and climbed out alone.

From where he stood on top of the trailer, he could see the ambulance and a police car just over a mile away, heading toward them.

Trevor climbed down and jogged over to the bank where Kaitlyn held the distraught woman in her arms. He sat next to Kaitlyn, putting his arm around them both.

"We should call your parents." He offered.

Kaitlyn froze. She didn't know if his words meant she would no longer get to be see her parents or not.

She nodded at him as he held out his own cell phone for her.

"Call them."

Kaitlyn took the phone with shaking hands and fumbled with the numbers until it began to ring.

"Hello?" her dad answered.

"Dad..." Kaitlyn felt a lump forming in her throat. The sound of her fathers' voice stabbed at her heart. She wanted to run to him and wrap her arms around him. "We were in an accident," she managed, feeling Trevor's eyes boring into her already aching skull. "I-"

Trevor snatched the phone from her.

"Mr. Hendricks. It's me, Trevor."

"Who? Trevor? I'll get to you in a second. I'd like to speak to my daughter. Put her back the phone."

Trevor could sense the frustration in his voice.

"Kaity is okay. She's got a concussion but no broken bones. The ambulance is just arriving. I'm not sure what hospital they will take us to. I can let you know as soon as they tell me."

"An accident? On the highway?" Mr. Hendricks asked.

"Yes sir. We are at mile marker 132."

"They will likely take you to Cook County medical center. If for some reason they don't, give us a call back. We will meet you there. Can I speak to Kaitlyn?"

Trevor could hear a woman's frantic voice asking about the accident in the background. Kaitlyn's mother.

"Daddy..." Kaitlyn pleaded for the phone.

He hung up as the ambulance stopped in front of them.

The paramedics rushed toward them, and Trevor stood, pulling Kaitlyn up with him. He wanted her examined first, within his supervision. As Kaitlyn took a step toward the medical team, she felt her head spin and footing give. Kaitlyn collapsed to the pavement before the team or Trevor could catch her.

"Kait!"

Two paramedics began assessing Kaitlyn's head injury and checking for others. Trevor was approached by a police officer who began asking a barrage of questions pertaining to the accident.

Kaitlyn was lifted on to a gurney and loaded into the ambulance.

Trevor continued to monitor Kaitlyn's state as he calmly answered the officers' questions.

Kaitlyn fluttered her eyes open as a Paramedic in a blue shirt began taking her blood pressure.

"Have you had anything to eat today?" he asked, while staring at his watch.

Kaitlyn saw her hand fly out and snatch the man's' arm. "Help me."

The paramedic nodded as the second paramedic stepped in. Kaitlyn reluctantly let loose of his sleeve as her head began to spin.

Trevor shoved his way into the ambulance and reached for Kaitlyn's hand.

Kaitlyn glanced up at her captor now gripping her hand tightly. Her eyes scanned the inside of the ambulance then out the open doors to see the older gentleman emerge from the overturned trailer. His face lined with deep sorrow, defeat and perhaps a little shame.

Kaitlyn recognized that look. It was exactly how Kaitlyn felt, her world completely overturned.

Chapter 22

Unstable

The Hendricks' paced the entrance of the emergency room, desperately waiting for the ambulance to arrive.

Not exactly the initial introduction Trevor had imagined.

Anxiety crept its way up his spine as he itched at the insides of his palms. This situation was a ticking time bomb. Trevor had carefully orchestrated Kaitlyn's encounters thus far, but now, his world suddenly felt threatened. He needed to be calm and cool.

Though this might just work in my favor.

Trevor gave the Hendricks half a smile as he followed the medical team into the Emergency room. Kaitlyn's mother tried to reach for her unconscious daughter, but the paramedics didn't stop. They pushed through the doors and down the hall. There was nothing she could do. The last time she had seen her daughter, she had been driving away happily.

"Mr. and Mrs. Hendricks?" Trevor asked as he approached. "I'm Trevor, your daughter's, uh, husband," he said sheepishly. "She's gonna be okay. She just needs some rest."

Kaitlyn's mother sighed in relief. Trevor smiled at her then held out a hand towards Kaitlyn's father. Frank Hendricks reluctantly met his hand and shook it.

Trevor seemed nothing like what he had pictured. This man appeared to be well dressed and well-mannered, perhaps even humble.

Kaitlyn's prior interests had been a bearded deadbeat and some guy on a motorcycle, obviously *not* good enough for his daughter.

"Call me Frank," he offered, "And this is Ellen."

"When can we see her?" Ellen asked.

"The doctors asked us to let her rest. She can have visitors after they have finished their examination." Trevor tried to hide the anxiety he felt knowing Kaitlyn could wake up at any minute and start weaving a nest of lies.

"So, what do we do now?" she asked, desperate.

"Wait. It's all we can do," Trevor said. Though not for too long, he hoped.

"You'd better get those cuts looked at," Ellen fussed as she pulled up Trevor's sleeve, revealing a clotted gash down the side of his forearm. "Come," she demanded, guiding him towards the nurse's station.

Minutes later the older couple from the accident were shuffled in. The lady on a gurney and the man following close behind.

Glancing up at Trevor, he stopped and stretched out his hand. Trevor took it and the man hugged him.

"I… I couldn't do it. Thank you," he choked.

"I'm sorry about your horses," Trevor replied.

"You are a good man. Your wife?" he asked. "How is she?"

Frank and Ellen stepped forward, listening to mans' words of commendation.

"She'll be fine."

The man nodded solemnly as he shuffled down the hall after this wife.

"Mr. Manning?" a nurse called from behind.

"Yes?"

"Your wife is awake."

Rushing into the room, Trevor saw Kaitlyn shifting in her hospital bed, her right eye slightly swollen and showing signs of discoloration. He sat on the bed next to her and held her hand.

"I'm here," he consoled.

"What happened?" she asked, a tremor of panic in her voice.

"You passed out. The doctors are going to keep you here for a little while. You have a mild concussion." He caressed the side of her face. "I have a surprise for you though."

Kaitlyn looked into his eyes, searching for sincerity.

"Your parents are here."

Her breath caught in her throat. *Is it true?*

"Oh baby!" her mother's voice called from the doorway as her parents entered the room.

"Oh honey, are you okay?"

Kaitlyn forced a smile as her mother sat on the side of her bed, taking her hand. Kaitlyn wrapped her arms around her mother and squeezed. A rush of emotions erupted from her chest, and she began sobbing uncontrollably. All she had wished for in the last couple months had been to see her mother again.

"Don't you worry. Your father and I will take care of everything. You just rest."

No, I will, Trevor thought to himself.

Ellen smoothed her daughter's hair affectionately. Kaitlyn nodded, then looked to her father standing at the doorway. He seemed concerned but dared not to show it.

A nurse rolled a cart into the room.

"Hey guys, I'm gonna have to ask you to give us a minute while I draw some blood for more tests."

Trevor felt his shoulders tighten. He had zero intention of leaving Kaitlyn alone any longer. He needed a plan.

"Sure," he nodded at the nurse. "It'll give your parents and me some time to talk." Trevor smiled coldly at Kaitlyn.

Kaitlyn glanced frantically from her mother to Trevor. She thought of the countless others Trevor had easily duped and convinced that she was mentally unstable. She couldn't let him do the same to her parents.

"No, mom, don't go," she pleaded, tightening her grip on her mother's arm.

"I'll stay," her mother agreed.

"Sorry ma'am, you must exit the room."

"But my daughter has just been in a terrible accident. She needs her mother," Ellen said firmly.

The nurse wouldn't budge.

Kaitlyn's hands began to tremble.

"Mom, don't leave. Please don't leave me."

Ellen sensed a desperation in her daughter's voice. Never before had she said those words. Hearing them now made her feel a sense of urgency.

Trevor stepped up and gently pulled Ellen away. The sight horrified Kaitlyn.

"It won't be long. We'll be right back," Trevor said, his tone glacial.

Guiding Frank and Ellen out of the room he ushered them to a quiet corner in the waiting area.

"I, uh, wanted to warn you two about something." Trevor ran his hands through his hair. "I really hoped to have more time before..."

"Before what?" Frank asked.

"Kaity isn't well."

Ellen gasped. "What is it?"

Trevor paused, waiting for them to lean in closer. Ellen placed a hand near her throat as she waited.

"She has been diagnosed with schizophrenia."

Ellen shook her head as the color drained from her face.

"What? I don't understand.... what is that exactly?"

Trevor went on, "It's a condition that messes with her mind, confuses her, makes her violent. She makes up these scenarios, believes them to be real, others fake. Until recently, she has even hurt herself."

Frank shook his head quietly in denial.

"Do you mean to tell me she's...suicidal?" Ellen asked timidly.

Trevor nodded, hiding behind a mask of shame. "I have tried to stop her. I have even been coming home from work to spend lunch with her, to keep an eye on her. But frankly, I am scared to leave her alone. That's why we were coming to visit you. I wanted her to talk to you two about it."

"About what? That she hurts herself?" Ellen said, appalled at the thought. "She would never do that!"

"That's what I thought too when I first met her. But she has a darker, secretive side. I'm sure you know she didn't even want me to meet you guys for so long."

He could tell he hit a nerve. Frank stiffened and looked at Ellen.

"There was that one year when we caught her sneaking out late at night. We thought maybe she was mixed up with a boy or doing drugs or something. She denied it of course and pulled away from us even more. Then she brought home the motorcycle guy. I don't remember his name but anyone that drives a motorcycle is trouble. What was she thinking...She wasn't? Her whole life she has tried to defy us and hide it."

Trevor found Mr. Hendricks statement interesting.

"Then you understand my frustration. I have nothing to hide. I don't know why she is trying to keep us apart. But I know one thing. She needs our help."

"Help?" Ellen asked.

"I contacted a doctor in town. He met with us on several occasions. He has recommended a short stay in a local facility for observation."

Trevor's words hung in the air like a thick fog.

Frank nodded. "How bad is it?"

"She thinks she doesn't know me."

Frank stepped forward. "She doesn't! And neither do we."

"Frank." Ellen gave him a stern look.

"Sorry, but something just doesn't seem right here. She never showed any signs in the past, then suddenly she has a condition?" Frank asked, looking directly at Trevor.

Frank didn't have to say it. Trevor knew he was being accused.

"I don't know what to say. All I know is she gets confused a lot, calling me names, and accusing me of things. I constantly tell her that I love her and am here for her. But she thinks I'm a monster." Trevor moved further into the waiting area, sat down on the sofa, and rubbed his face in his hands. He noticed that neither Ellen nor Frank was quick to comfort him.

"I don't want her committed. I have been trying so hard to keep her safe and happy and watch over her myself. I really don't know what else to do."

"I just can't believe our little girl is going *crazy*. I just can't." Frank disagreed.

"Don't! Don't call her crazy. She is *not* crazy, she is just... confused. And we are going to find out what is really going on and help her!" Ellen said.

"So, what do we do?" Frank asked, putting his arm around Ellen.

Ellen took a deep breath and gazed up at Trevor with earnest searching eyes.

"We are her parents; she is our responsibility. We will get her the finest doctors in the country."

"Maybe seeing you will help her?" Trevor offered, feeling he was on the verge of losing control of the situation.

He needed a new approach.

Frank wanted nothing more than to march back into the room and hear his daughter's side. He had enough of what this man was telling them. But something stopped him.

"Or it might push her over the edge. We didn't have the best relationship before she moved," Frank admitted.

"Really?" Trevor asked, feigning surprise. "She always spoke so highly of you two," he added, knowing that comment would melt their hearts a little.

Ellen smiled and rubbed Frank's arm.

That was the moment Frank knew Trevor was lying.

Kaitlyn watched as the nurse withdrew a syringe and several empty vials.

"Can you help me?" Kaitlyn whispered, glancing at the doorway. "I need to get out of here."

The nurse stopped for a moment and then continued with her

work.

"Please. That man out there is not my husband. He kidnapped me!"

The nurse raised an eyebrow as she plunged the needle into Kaitlyn's arm.

"You don't believe me, I know. Trevor probably told you I am crazy or something, and he got that doctor to write a letter saying I need to be committed to a mental hospital, but it's all lies. Please, you've got to help me!"

"Who is Trevor?" the nurse asked.

"My husband, or the one saying he is my husband! He is telling lies about me!"

"So, the guy you just said wasn't your husband, is also the one telling lies about you?"

"Yes."

"I think I understand. Your husband kidnapped you?" she asked skeptically.

"He is *not* my husband!" Kaitlyn shouted, wrenching her arm from the nurse.

The nurse quickly gathered up her vials. "Mrs. Manning, I don't want to restrain you. Please lay back so I can finish-"

"I'm not Mrs. Manning! My name is Kaitlyn Hendricks! I want to see my parents!" Kaitlyn shoved the sheets off her legs and scrambled to her feet.

The nurse hit an emergency button near the wall and an alarm sounded down the hall. Two orderlies rushed in.

"The patient is unstable and showing signs of aggression."

The men grabbed Kaitlyn and pulled her back to the bed.

Trevor and her parents ran in as Kaitlyn was forcibly strapped to her bed, fighting the entire time.

Rushing to her side, Trevor smoothed the hair from her face.

"Baby, you need to calm down. These people are here to help you. We are *all* here to help you."

Trevor kissed the side of her cheek.

She had had enough of that. Her eyes darted to her parents, standing in utter shock. She realized Trevor had likely poisoned them against her.

Trevor squeezed himself between the orderlies, burying his smile in her hair as he comforted her. She was reacting better than he had hoped.

"Perhaps I should call Dr. Putten," Trevor said.

Kaitlyn's eyes widened. Her parents looked at each other, perplexed. To them, it was a harmless suggestion.

"Yes, baby. It might be good if he came to see you."

Kaitlyn swallowed hard. "I don't want to talk to him. I want to talk to my parents! Alone!"

The nurse sighed, having finally finished drawing Kaitlyn's blood. She gestured to the orderlies and they both excused themselves.

"I'll give you a moment," Trevor offered graciously.

The sight of Trevor leaving should have given Kaitlyn respite, but she knew she had very little time to convince her parents of the truth. And, she had to choose her words carefully.

"Daddy," Kaitlyn grasped for words as tears welled up in her eyes. She wondered where to start.

She hadn't called him that in years.

"Oh sweetheart, don't cry. We are right here," Frank consoled.

Kaitlyn shook her head. "I need to get away from that man," she whispered.

"Trevor?" Ellen asked.

"He kidnapped me."

Frank and Ellen glanced at each other warily. "Tell us everything," her father said.

"He was one of the movers. I thought he was nice. We got lunch together. When we came back, they finished setting up my apartment and I thought that was it."

Kaitlyn remembered that day so vividly. Her excitement upon looking at her otherwise barren apartment so open to possibility. *How naïve I was then, believing I was free.*

"I thought I was on my own. It happened so fast. He must have been hiding the entire time. He grabbed hold of me and locked me in my room. He... he did terrible things." she swallowed back a sob as the words passed her lips. "He never lets me out of his sight unless he is at work. Otherwise, he chains me up, or he drugs me." Her emotions took over as she began to sob uncontrollably, clinging to her mother's arms.

Ellen was horrified, peering through the doorway behind her as if looking back at the man she just met, a man she realized she knew nothing about. She rubbed Kaitlyn's shoulder as they listened.

"And he somehow thinks we're married, that we're in love and meant to be together. He's insane! Worst of all, Trevor wants *me* committed to a mental hospital."

Frank paced the room momentarily. It felt too much to take in.

Frank began to wonder about the letters and about a sudden

wedding she had without their knowledge of the boy or even an invite.

There was no way she could have kept that from us for so long, along with her "condition."

Frank thought about how Trevor talked to them, tried to convince them that their daughter needed psychiatric help. Frank felt his hands ball into fists.

"Why do *you* think he wants to have you committed?" he asked.

"I don't know, but he does."

Trevor re-entered the room, his face smug. Frank stepped forward. He would not let him go near his daughter. Just then, the nurse pushed her way in between them.

"Doctor has ordered a sedative," she said, bringing forth the needle.

"No! I hate being drugged, please don't!" Kaitlyn shouted, trying to jerk her arm away.

It was too late. The syringe had plunged the liquid into her veins faster than she could react.

A second nurse entered the room.

"I don't want to be drugged. I'm tired of all the drugs!"

The two nurses glanced at each other.

"Is that really necessary?" Ellen asked, feeling helpless as she watched her daughter drift away.

"I'm afraid it is," the second nurse asserted.

Frank watched Trevor the entire time. Trevor could feel the eyes on him and met his stare.

"You okay, Mr. Hendricks?" he asked.

Frank wanted nothing more than to pummel him into the ground. But he knew this wasn't the time or the place. He had to be sure.

"I keep thinking about this thing she told me, about you chaining her up. It sounded so ludicrous. Must be another one of her delusions, right?" Frank questioned.

Trevor could detect the anger in his voice.

He realized he might not be able to persuade Frank after all. He wouldn't need to. Weather the Hendricks' believed him or not, it was no long up to them. As Kaitlyn's husband, Trevor had sole authority to decide what was best for Kaitlyn.

"Right you are. She lays in bed all day, every day. She stays inside the apartment, nothing more. Dr. Putten could only do so much, which is why he recommended admitting her."

Frank decided to call Trevor's bluff. "I would like to hear from this doctor myself. I think he's the only one capable of making a decision regarding her…condition."

Trevor wanted to laugh aloud. Dr. Putten, a man he briefly met at a party, whose wife he had fooled around with, had ended up becoming his greatest resource

"I'll call him," Trevor said, then abruptly left the room.

Ellen waited until she could no longer hear Trevor's footsteps.

"What are we going to do, Frank?"

"We're going to hear exactly what this doctor has to say."

Frank walked over to his daughter's bedside, recalling the way she screamed at the sight of the needle, how she fought the nurses yet looked at Trevor the whole time. He reached for his daughter's hand, grasping as lightly as he could.

"Then Trevor will hear what I have to say."

Chapter 23

Guardianship

Dr. Putten marched down the hall of Cook County Medical Center to room B103.

As Roger rounded the corner, he spotted Trevor, leaning against the wall with his arms folded over his chest.

"I came as soon as I could. Anything new?" Roger asked.

"The physician on duty ordered a sedative. She has been pretty upset."

Inside, Dr. Putten found Kaitlyn's parents sitting on either side of their daughter's bed.

Roger introduced himself as Kaitlyn's doctor. Neither of her parents responded. He did not feel welcome.

Ellen simply nodded. Frank reluctantly rose to meet him.

"I'm Frank Hendricks. Thank you for coming."

"Of course. How is she?"

"We were hoping you could tell us," Ellen said.

"I guess I'll cut to the chase. I suggested to Trevor that Kaitlyn seek professional care. I can't disclose the details, but Kaitlyn has called me on several occasions asking for help, which is good. She *wants* to get better, and, at times, recognizes she needs help."

Dr. Putten opened his briefcase, rummaging through his files. He held out a slip.

"Here is an official order for your daughter to be moved to a mental health care facility. She will be under my direct supervision."

Frank extended the document to Ellen and Frank. They read it over and over, flipping it back and forth. It was legitimate but didn't explain *everything*.

"Now, this isn't my usual manner of practice. I do a lot of counseling and weekly monitoring of my current patients, but for Trevor, I agreed to oversee Kaitlyn's care myself."

Just then, the doctor on duty entered the room. Dr. Putten shook hands with Dr. North, exchanging credentials.

"Thank you, Roger, for coming in."

Dr. North glanced at Kaitlyn, half conscious on the bed. He started to say something but stopped before anyone noticed.

"No problem, Greg. It's just a little favor for the family."

"There is something we should discuss," Dr. Greg North stole another look at Kaitlyn again and then lowered his voice. "Her test results came back, and we found something." He handed Roger the file and the two men shared a knowing look.

"Well," Roger retrieved a paper from his open briefcase and handed it over. "Now, you won't have to worry about that. I am assuming her care, and Trevor here will be her guardian. I will discuss this with him."

Dr. Greg North glanced back at Kaitlyn for a moment then narrowed his eyes at Trevor.

"What? What is it?" Ellen demanded.

Kaitlyn stirred and turned her head toward the voices. Once she opened her eyes and saw Dr. North, she tried to pull herself upright.

"What is *he* doing here?"

"It's just your doctor, sweetheart." Ellen shushed her daughter.

"Well, I'll expect a report included in this reassignment," Dr. North said to Dr. Putten as he turned toward the door.

"Don't leave me..." Kaitlyn whispered to Dr. North.

He sighed, avoiding her gaze, then shook hands with Frank and nodded at Ellen before he excused himself.

"What was that all about?" Trevor asked as he leaned in close to Dr. Putten. Frank had his eyes on them.

"I'm afraid Trevor and I need to talk privately," Dr. Putten said, gesturing toward the door.

It was not what Frank wanted to hear.

"We are her parents, damn it! We deserve to know! She barely knew this guy." Frank demanded.

Roger winced. He finally understood the situation in the room.

"Just, one moment, Mr. Hendricks," he said calmly. Roger then led the way out.

They made their way to the reception area down the hall.

"What is it?" Trevor asked, feeling anxious.

Roger looked all around him, making sure what he was about to say was for Trevor's ears only.

"Did you know she was pregnant?" Roger asked under his breath.

Trevor's eyes widened. He took a steadying breath.

"Pregnant? Really?" Trevor began to pace the area wildly. "No, I didn't." He shook his head as he processed the news. "We had talked about trying, but with all that was going on, we sort of dropped it."

"Well, congratulations, you are going to be a father. But let me warn you. She is in the very early stages and a lot can happen in the first trimester. I don't want you going out and buying baby stuff just yet."

Trevor stopped. "She might lose it?"

"Well, that *is* a possibility, with everything she has been through, plus her mental state. That leads me to our next discussion. I gather you *want* this baby. So, in order to protect that little life from its mother and her...let's say, mood swings, then we need to take measures to ensure both of their safety."

"Anything. What do we need to do?"

"I need your permission to request a heavily sedated state for the term of her pregnancy to ensure she will be unable to hurt herself or her unborn child," Roger said solemnly.

"Of course. What do you need from me?"

"Just your permission as her guardian and the child's guardian."

Trevor couldn't hide his smile. He had won.

"I'm her guardian?"

"Yes, of course. Why wouldn't you be? You *are* her husband. From here on out you will be making all her decisions. Her care is solely under your guardianship, though I am sure you will want to include her parents in any decisions you make."

Trevor nodded, taking it all in. "I can handle that. Let's go tell her parents about the baby."

Roger led the way, stopping at the doorway upon the sight of Frank, who had grown increasingly impatient. Roger stepped aside.

"You first," he said to Trevor.

Chapter 24

The Lake

Kaitlyn stared out the window from her hospital bed. The view beyond was nothing like the lake she had grown accustomed to. The desolate parking lot filled with cars coming and going offered zero comfort. Her room, now a sterile, cold tomb in which she imagined she would die, seemed to shrink every day.

The facility she now resided in, was no hospital. It was in fact, a mental asylum. She had overheard her parents call it a clinic.

Kaitlyn had wanted to laugh at the statement, but the sedatives pulsing through her veins numbed her senses and robbed her of her will to fight.

She wondered how many more lies Trevor had told to convince her parents and everyone ells that she belonged there.

Her belly grew every day as doctors checked on her, more concerned with the little life inside her than hers.

She tried to swallow back the reality of Trevor's control over the new little soul. Half of the time she wished it gone for its own sake.

The other half, she felt overjoyed to be part of something new and pure. She promised herself and the baby that she would do all in her power to see that Trevor had nothing to do with its little life.

Kaitlyn replayed the moment Dr. Roger Putten told her she was pregnant. She had known all along but feared Trevor would use it against her. Now she lay in the hospital bed, starring at the ceiling, listening to the rhythmic sound of the monitoring equipment.

Kaitlyn closed her eyes and imagined she could see the lake, with a pair of loons gliding across effortlessly, leaving a ripple trailing behind them. She watched how the ripples on the glassy water spread out across the lake, all while the loons held their heads up high.

I will do whatever it takes. she promised herself, *I will keep you safe.*

Perhaps we are safe? she wondered. *No more hurting, no more danger from Trevor.*

He had been to see her every week. But he could not hurt her. She was safe in the care of the people in white coats. Though she was constantly reminded that she had no control of her own.

Her greatest fear had enveloped her and now she lay alone in her white prison. She wondered if there was any hope of her returning to her former life.

Her parents came once a week, though they never stayed long. The regular drugs she was subjected to, clouded her judgment, and confused her thoughts as she tried her best to convey the danger, she had been in. She had given them the bullet points of her kidnapping and the struggles that she endured.

Though they spoke of believing her, neither of them seemed to have the authority to remove her from her confinement.

Their relationship had grown over the months, and they had expressed their regret for trying to control every aspect of her adult life, even scaring away her one true love. Kaitlyn thought about him for a moment, his clear green eyes, his light brown hair. She wondered if he even cared that she had been committed to a mental facility.

She had broken his heart. He sold his motorcycle to please her, but then left town when she hesitated to have a secret relationship with him.

Kaitlyn glanced down at her hand resting on her belly. She longed to tell him everything and feel his comforting arms wrap around her. But that wouldn't happen now.

She recalled seeing him, his eyes had been cold and judging. No love or care left.

"How's my pumpkin?" Trevor called as he entered her room.

Kaitlyn hated being called a pumpkin. She knew it was because her belly was showing. And Trevor loved to call her nicknames. At least here she didn't have to pretend to be his wife anymore. She didn't have to speak to him or answer his questions. She could just close her eyes and picture the lake. Because sooner or later she'd get what she wanted; Trevor to leave.

"Doc says you only got 3 weeks to go. Baby is in the clear. We are home free now."

Home, Kaitlyn wondered. *Where is home exactly?*

"We scored a big client and now our business is making bank, babe. I am doing my best to keep up. It fills the lonely nights at home when I am not working at the clinic.

"Roger and Tammy left on a three-month vacation, so it's been kind of lonely around the park. They should be home in a couple weeks I think." Trevor hated being ignored by her. His fists balled as he went on.

"I'm spending the holidays at your parents. I wish you could be with us. They talk about you a lot," he knew that would hit a nerve with her, but she sat with her eyes closed and no change of expression. "Look at me!" he shouted then quickly replaced his scowl with a fake smile as an orderly walked past the door.

Trevor moved to the side of her bed and laid his hand on her belly.

Kaitlyn opened her eyes and looked at him for the first time in a long time. He looked tired, even a bit drawn. Her rage toward him had long since transformed to unrelenting determination.

She was no longer angry. She knew that anger held a person back. What she had now was pure driven desire to see him suffer until he succumbed to a painful death. He had conned his way into her life. That was *his* mistake.

She thought of what he said and concealed a smile. She knew he was lying. Her parents were well informed of his true self and would not for one second welcome him into their house. He was losing control.

"I thought of some names. Junior if it's a boy. Sara if it's a girl. What do you think?"

Trevor had made a habit of constantly asking. Kaitlyn was used to it, and blankly tuned him out.

While Trevor shuffled through a set a drawer, Kaitlyn stole a quick glance at him. He looked terrible. His hair was thinning, his cheeks hollow and his eyes bloodshot.

Trevor felt her scrutiny and shifted uncomfortably as he ran a hand through his hair.

"What?" he shouted at her. He rubbed at his leg as he glared at her. "Don't look at me like that."

Kaitlyn continued to stare blankly at him. She knew this drove him crazy. Every time he lost control; she felt a little freer.

Trevor pushed his anger and self loathing to the side and returned his fake happy persona to its usual place as he got to his feet.

"I am gonna stop in at your parents before I." Trevor stumbled as he stepped toward the door. He glanced up at Kaitlyn in desperation. "I..." he stammered as he fell to the floor.

Kaitlyn watched as her captor laid on the floor writhing in pain. She *could* call for help. She had a button just inches from her hand. Instead, she watched him hurt.

Perhaps he is sick? She wondered with no concern.

Kaitlyn could see it. *Something... something terrible and rotten had formed inside him.*

Whatever it was, she was grateful. She had prayed for the day she could watch him writhe in pain. And now she was be granted her prayer.

"Kait, call for help. I can't get up. Kait!" Trevor pleaded.

Several minutes passed as Kaitlyn watched in awed horror at Trevor's convulsions and suffering before a nurse popped his head in and saw Trevor on the floor.

The nurse hit the emergency call button and crouched over Trevor taking his vitals and then another nurse rushed in.

"He's breathing, but his pulse is erratic. Get the crash cart."

The second nurse rushed out as a third rushed in.

Kaitlyn watched in enamored silence as the white coats busied themselves over their new patient on the floor. Trevor cried out in agony.

A stretcher was brought in. As the nurses maneuvered him onto the gurney, Trevor howled in pain, his face twisting, warping.

For the first time, she saw the *real* Trevor. A lost and scared little boy who only wanted his mother.

Kaitlyn suddenly wished she could stand over him and tell him he was getting every ounce of pain he deserved.

Trevor's screams echoed down the hall as he was rolled out of her room.

Kaitlyn smiled slightly as she returned her gaze to her imaginary view just beyond the window, the lake.

Chapter 25

Diagnosis

Trevor stewed with frustration and contempt. He balled his fists and thrust them down on the mattress beside his traitorous leg. He had run out of time. The cancer had taken hold of him, consuming him from the inside out.

The bone cancer had taken over his right leg. He had been told he needed a bone marrow transplant.

Such a simple solution, but not a single donor provided a match.

Trevor recalled the moment he laid eyes on Kaitlyn. She had happened to walk into the clinic the same very same day he decided he was done waiting. He was sick of waiting to die.

A plan began forming in his mind. A child of his *own* could provide him with the life saving marrow. He just needed someone he could persuade; someone he could *control*.

At first, he chose Kaitlyn out of the need to survive. But there had been more than that. He desired her. The way she smiled, the way she walked, so innocent, so unaware of the world.

Trevor growled under his breath. He was so close, yet in so much pain.

"Do something!" he shouted at the nurses.

Dr. Greg North entered the room, clipboard in hand. "I think you know what I am about to say."

Trevor nodded in dismay. He refused to give in.

"It doesn't look good. The cancer cells have spread at an alarming rate. Without an immediate donor you could be looking at a few weeks at best."

That was all he needed. He had beaten the odds before.

"What if I had a match?" Trevor asked. "Then what?"

"We would get you in for surgery right away. But so far, we don't."

"I do. But I would need a few weeks."

Dr. North folded his arms. "What are you talking about?"

Trevor took a deep breath.

"I have a child. He or she could be born in a few weeks. It is my only living flesh and blood, and a guaranteed match."

The doctor scoffed. "Are you suggesting we take a bone marrow transplant from your newborn child? Do you know the risks involved?"

Dr. North glared at his patient. "Besides, I don't think we have that kind of time. You'd need it now if there is a chance it could take."

Trevor winced as he tried to sit up. "My wife and child are under my guardianship. My wife, as *you* know, is unwell. She is at that mental hospital and never getting out."

Dr. North shook his head at Trevor. "I cannot believe a father would suggest such a thing."

Trevor fumed. If only he had his syringe and make this doctor do as he said.

"Induce the labor and take the child now!"

"In all the history of evil, self-preserving bastards, you sir, take the cake. The risk of the procedure alone, plus an early birth on top of it. I can't guarantee we could extract enough marrow from a newborn to make a dent in your situation." The doctor marched toward the door shaking his head.

"Please," Trevor begged.

"I'm sorry, but I refuse to take that kind of risk for patient or for my license."

"I want that bone marrow! I'll get a judge's order if I must!"

"Then I will see to it that you lose guardianship over your Kaitlyn and the baby."

Snatching up the closest thing within reach, Trevor hurled a clip board at the doctor, just missing him, and cracking against the door jam.

"I refuse to lay here and wait to die!" he shouted as she reached for the phone on the side table.

"Hey baby." Trevor called to her.

Startled from her sleep, Kaitlyn glanced towards the voice. Suddenly she realized she was in an unfamiliar room. Her hospital bed now sharing a room with Trevor.

"What's this?" Kaitlyn whispered half to herself.

"We are getting ready to have a baby, baby!"

"Don't call me that." she said.

"Oh, don't be sore," he cooed. "You are saving my life!"

"I won't let you take my baby," she spat.

"It's done," he said flatly. "Besides, it wasn't my decision. It's all in your parents' hands now."

The nurse left them alone, closing the door behind her.

"You are the devil himself aren't you."

"No. I am your husband and the father of that child. That child is going to save my life. Can't you at least be happy for me, for us?"

Kaitlyn retreated into herself. She was done giving him the satisfaction of conversation.

"Ok, Mrs. Manning." Dr. North said as he entered the room. "Are you ready to have this baby?"

Kaitlyn glared, stone-faced to his inquiry. She hated being called Mrs. Manning, *especially by him*. There was nothing to be said.

Trevor continued to rule over her just as he had since the beginning.

Trevor rambled on in the distance, but Kaitlyn focused on the scene beyond the window. Her scene, not the drab winter gloom, but the lake in her mind that comforted her. She pictured the blackness of the water as it reflected every flickering sparkle from the stars above to her beloved town below.

"Why did you do this?" she heard herself say.

Surprised by her sudden decision to speak to him, he rolled to face her. She wouldn't look at him as she stared at the window.

"Why *me*? What was all this for?" she asked again.

"I needed you."

Kaitlyn nodded her head, waiting for him to go on.

"I needed someone to have my child, someone I could trust."

Kaitlyn wanted to laugh out loud, but her throat was too tight from the anxiety of her eminent birth

"This child is literally saving my life."

Trevor waited nervously. His salvation only minutes away, yet another feeling began to ache in his stomach.

Trevor let his head fall back against his pillow. The ceiling offered little consolation. A blank white nothingness looming above.

He was about to get everything he had wanted and planned for.

Kaitlyn and a clear plastic basinet where wheeled into Trevor's hospital room.

No turning back now, Trevor ruminated. The plan he had initiated nearly a year ago had brought him to this moment.

Trevor's thoughts were interrupted as Dr. North entered the room. His expression eerily intrigued.

"I have some news for you," the doctor said.

"Yeah?"

"Well, first of all, you should know that the child was born successfully at seven pounds, four ounces."

Something in Dr. North's tone seemed off to Trevor. He appeared arrogant, even amused.

"Your scans from yesterday show a significant pocket around the back side of your brain. Near the Sympathetic Nervous System." Dr. North cleared his throat. I have spoken with your Oncologist and it seems your cancer is aggressively spreading." Dr. North moved closer.

"As a standard procedure to determine the donor is indeed a match...." Dr. North rounded the bed and stood directly beside Trevor, gazing down at him. "It seems, Mr. Manning, the bone marrow of the child is *not* a match. That led me to a DNA test. And it is fairly conclusive. Child is not *your son* after all."

Trevor's head began to spin. His world felt like quicksand under him. *Am I sinking?*

"How? How could that be? She hasn't been with *anyone* but me! I didn't even let her out of my sight!" his voice began to raise. "This is impossible!" Trevor shouted trying to lift himself from the bed.

"Out of your sight?" the doctor asked.

"Check it again. That *is* my child. It has to be!" Trevor barked. "The child is everything, my whole plan!"

Doctor North stepped back and looked at Trevor as if for the first time.

"So, she has been telling the truth..."

Overhearing the commotion, Kaitlyn struggled to swallow back the nausea, determined to understand exactly what the doctor and Trevor were yelling about.

"It seems you are out of time, and as of this moment, no longer have authority over the infant or Kaitlyn."

Trevor blinked at Dr. North. *This isn't happening. It can't be.*

"I guess I will leave you to it then."

"Leave me to what?!" Trevor cried.

"To your fate," the doctor replied coldly. "There is nothing we can do for you."

Kaitlyn looked from her child to Trevor across the room and then back to her child. Had Dr. North believed her?

She had told him how she had been kidnapped, drugged, and

made out to be some delusional woman. She had pleaded for help, but not one of them listened. Except Dr. Greg North. He had been the only one.

She pressed the call button for the nurse, never taking her eyes off Trevor.

The nurses popped her head in. "Need something?"

"Yes." Kaitlyn smiled for the first time in a long time. "May I hold my baby?" she asked.

The nurse handed Kaitlyn her swaddled little soul.

She pressed the warm bundle to her chest and closed her eyes. Her son was warm and perfect. Her heart began to swell with joy. *Of course,* she thought to herself. *This perfect little soul had nothing to do with Trevor!*

This sudden realization meant her son had a future, a life to live. It meant freedom for them both!

Chapter 26

The End

Trevor stared at the ceiling feeling numb and cold. His days were numbered, hours in fact. His mask of deception had cracked. Shattered.

Kaitlyn moved to a private room where both her and the baby would be free from Trevor for good.

A nurse in light blue scrubs strolled in.

Trevor barely noticed her.

"You've got a visitor," the nurse said.

Trevor scoffed into his pillow. The bone crushing ache in his leg had spread to his spine. Every movement, breath and twitch of his muscles radiated fire beneath his skin. He hated the body that continued to betray him.

He glanced over his shoulder, curiosity getting the better of him. There in a yellow dress stood Tammy Putten. She tiptoed up to the bed.

"I didn't want to wake you," she whispered. "We heard you were ill, so we cut our vacation a little short."

"Really?" Trevor sat up feeling surprised and slightly embarrassed. "Why?"

"Well..." she said, glancing down.

Trevor suddenly noticed she was holding her belly. There she stood, pregnant and glowing with as much joy as any proud mother-to-be could contain.

"Are you?" Trevor couldn't spit out the words. He wanted to throw up.

"Yes!" she giggled.

"Yes, we are!" Roger stated flatly as he waltzed into the room. "We uh, well. I didn't want to water down your special day. We just saw your little one down the hall. Congratulations."

Trevor grunted. Something about Rogers mood piqued his curiosity.

"We wanted to thank you," Roger added.

"We tried for years." Tammy added sheepishly.

"Thank you so much. You gave us what *I* couldn't. I guess we cashed in those favors." he said with a sheepish smile.

"We are so happy! Only 3 weeks to go!" Tammy giggled.

Trevor lay silent, trying to comprehend it all.

"Trevor. You gave me this baby, gave *us* this baby." Tammy said, grabbing Roger's hand. "We have wanted to be parents for years, but..."

"But it was impossible," Roger said. "Then *you* came along."

A loud hum began to form in Trevor's ears. Had Roger been eagerly helping with Kaitlyn because he felt he owed him for the conception? The hum in Trevor's head began to grow louder and louder until the room seemed to shake from the reverb of the sound.

The entire time, he thought, *Tammy was playing me! They all were!*

Dr. North entered the room with a concerned look.

Trevor watched as Tammy and Roger Putten were ushered out of the room, along with his only chance of life. It was the cruelest joke. He wanted to laugh but the vibration in his head consumed him.

Trevor blinked feeling the rush of cold blanketing his limbs. *This is it,* he thought. *This end.*

Dr. North stood over his patients. One lifeless monster, abandoning the world with no time to spare. The other he held in his arms, fresh and pure and innocent.

Dr. Greg North held his son in his hands wondering how Kaitlyn had strayed so far from him in the last year.

He had regretted every moment of his fight with Kaitlyn nine months ago. The one that had prompted him to leave town, taking a position at Cook County.

He had barely recognized Kaitlyn when she was first brought in after the car accident. Keeping his personal involvement with Kaitlyn a secret so she would not be removed from his care.

It would take time to for Kaitlyn to heal from her experience, but he had a feeling that the little soul in his arms would help her recovery.

Dr. Greg North flipped off the light as he left Trevor's lifeless body in the room.

"Have Mr. and Mrs. Hendricks informed of their daughters release," he said, strolling down the hall with the child in his arms.

Kaitlyn clutched her child to her breast as Greg sat beside her on the bed.

"What are you gonna call him?" he asked tentatively, feeling inner guilt for not doing more to help his former lover.

Kaitlyn inhaled the infant's thin tuft of black hair. A nurse had informed her of Trevor's passing moments before. She had cried tears of vindication and joy.

Now she held her baby, with Greg eager to acquire her release. A single tear traced her face as she smiled.

"Gregory," she said, fighting back the tears. "I want to name him Gregory."

About the Author

Trace devoured the works of Dan Brown, Michael Crichton, Gillian Flynn, John Grisham, and many others during her early years. Her flair for the adventure and heart pumping thrills has become the foundation for her writing. Action-packed thrillers with unexpected twists, conspiracy, and a taste of the dark side of love, all weave through her novels as her complex characters reveal a tiny bit of what is really hiding deep down inside of us all.

Trace has spent her adult life traveling and exploring the variety of cultures and architecture throughout Europe. Her education in architecture and art history have given her writing depth and art-istry as she describes narrow cobble stone alleys in Venice, librar-ies in Prague, or unearthed pyramids across the globe.

Her endeavor to experience new adventures has taken her from one extreme to the next, receiving training in such fields as Fire-arms, Repelling, Fencing, Martial Arts, and Archeology.

Her sweeter, softer, more feminine side invites the ocean breeze on a sailing excursion to the Grecian Isles, or wine tasting her way across Paris to Siena during one of her writing adventures. And of course, cooking pasta with the local Italians, is just one of the perks.

Trace Noir leads a far from normal life as a writer. On any given day, she can usually be found with a glass of wine in her hand and a smile on her face. She is confident in her skills and, constantly challenging herself. A typical "Tom-Boy" as she was affectionately called growing up in Alaska, Trace loves her "girl" clothes and her shoes, to the point of wearing her heels to the gun range, the beach, the movies, or just simply to wash her car on a Sunday morning.

Due to all the adventures and high paced activities, she is routinely asked, "Do you sleep?" And her answer is always, "Yes! Very well. Thank you."

When asked about her role as an author she states, "I write what I would like to watch at the movies. It should be fast paced, interesting, and full of deceit. I like a story to be thrilling, action-packed, and mysterious. I love a hint of science fiction and conspiracy tangled in a mystery. It must have a love triangle or forbidden passion. And the bad guy, needs to win at least some of the time."

"When I write, I pull from my own life's experiences and build on them. I see every word I type as it might be interpreted and visualized on a screen."

"I may be a new author on the scene, but I have a *seasoned* mind when it comes to knowing what makes a gripping tale."

Check out other Books by Trace Noir

www.TraceNoir.com

www.ingramcontent.com/pod-product-compliance
Lightning Source LLC
Chambersburg PA
CBHW070815120626
46556CB00002B/508